Raven in the Wind

Who was Woden? Was he god or man? His courage, exploits, wisdom and strength, won him a special place in the hearts of the Anglo-Saxon peoples and he became a legendary figure.

As with Adonis of the Greeks, Priapus of the Romans, Osiris of the Egyptians, Baldur of the Scandinavians, Jesus of the Christians, and others worshipped as gods, Woden's story was that of a beautiful male whose mystical beginnings were linked with a time of unrest, who suffered a bloody wound, died and was resurrected. Were these supermen the symbols of a fertility cult in which death and return mirrored the seasonal death and revival of nature? Were they central figures in a magical rite to ensure the return of a fruitful season? Whatever their significance, whence did they come?

This, the story of Woden, is the prologue to the author's Wyatt Saga.

The Howard Saga

Maid of Gold
Like As the Roaring Waves
The Queen's Fourth Husband
Lion Without Claws
Yet A Lion

The Wyatt Saga

Lord of the Black Boar
Sword of Woden
Tree of Vortigern
The Atheling
The Master of Blandeston Hall
The Heir of Allington
Sound Now the Passing-bell
The Knight of Allington
The Rebel of Allington
My Lute Be Still

Philippa Wiat

Raven in the Wind

ROBERT HALE · LONDON

© *Philippa Wiat 1978*
First published in Great Britain 1978

ISBN 0 7091 6561 7

Robert Hale Limited
Clerkenwell House
Clerkenwell Green
London EC1R oHT

Printed in Great Britain by
Clarke, Doble & Brendon Ltd,
Plymouth and London

To Dennis with Love

"Venus, in sport, to please therewith her dear,
Did on the helm of mighty Mars the red.
His spear she took, his targe she might not steer;
She looked as though her foes should all be dead,
So wantonly she frowneth with her cheer.
Priapus gan smile and said: 'Do way for dread,
Do way, madame, these weapons great and grim.
I, I for you am weapon fit and trim.' "

SIR THOMAS WYATT

PART I

THE ARRIVAL

ONE

Earl Leofgar was dying. He was very old and very wise. But he was not beloved of the gods. A long time ago, in his wild and reckless youth, he had slain his elder brother. His brother, lord of the Anglian tribe who dwelt in the burgh of Angel, had been cruel and merciless but the gods had not found it in their hearts to forgive Leofgar his one transgression, for loyalty to one's lord and one's kin surpassed all other considerations. After his brother's death, Leofgar had become chieftain of his people, the tribe had grown and prospered under his leadership as it would never have done under his brother's leadership, but still the curse of the gods lay upon him.

Leofgar had no son. Three wives he had had, but the gods had taken his first two wives in childbed, together with his still-born sons. When his second wife had died, Leofgar had been old—old as the Angles judged old, and old as the gods judged old. In his sixty-sixth winter then, Leofgar had needed a son to succeed him. He had taken another wife, a comely young woman, the daughter of a neighbouring Anglian chieftain, and nine months afterwards she too had died in childbed, but not before she had given Leofgar his first living child, a daughter he had named Ricole.

Leofgar's heart was heavy within him as he lay on his death-bed, alone but for his beloved Ricole. The gods had never ceased to vent their wrath upon him. He had given his people stability, he had ruled them with wisdom and firmness, but he was well aware that his day was nearly done. Without him to control the wild young warriors, his people would be at their mercy and, torn asunder by strife and dissension, by greed and the desire for power, by men who lacked a strong leader, the tribe would rapidly revert to its savage state. Without a son to succeed him, without an obvious and undisputed heir to take his place, the leadership would without doubt fall finally into the hands of the most unworthy and unscrupulous of the warriors.

"Alas, my father, I fear you are sorely troubled," Ricole said gently, breaking in upon Leofgar's thoughts.

"I am, my child," Leofgar admitted. "I am concerned for the future well-being of our people."

Ricole placed a comforting hand on his arm. "I pray you rest, my father. You can do no more—the future of our people lies with the gods."

Leofgar watched her in silence for a few moments, his fears temporarily lulled by her serenity. It seemed to him then that the gods, whilst denying him the sons he so urgently needed, had shown, by giving him Ricole—the fruit of his aged loins, whose beauty surpassed that of every other woman he had ever seen—that they were not totally devoid of mercy for him.

Ricole's hair was long and lustrous and white-gold in colour, her eyes were greenish-blue like the sea on the shore on a clear day, her skin was fair and flawless, and her body was supple and graceful with the blossoming curves of young maidenhood. Ricole's beauty was matched by her gentleness and serenity, and by the loving kindness she showed to all who came within her orbit.

Leofgar sighed, his fears returning. Was not Ricole's beauty, her gentleness, more of a curse than a blessing? He had observed the covetous gaze of his warriors upon her, he had seen the lust in their eyes; just as he had seen

Ricole's unawareness of their salacious glances, her childlike innocence and faith in the inherent goodness of Man.

"What of your future, Ricole?" Leofgar asked. "Who will protect you when I am gone?"

"Protect me, father? Protect me from what?" Ricole smiled. "Am I not among my own people? Am I not the daughter of their lord? I have uncles, I have cousins, have I not? All will protect me."

"Do you not see the lust you arouse in the minds of men, my child?"

"Lust, father?" Ricole asked, in surprise.

"Once I am dead, daughter, my warriors will quarrel over you. Already Cerdic has asked me for your hand in marriage."

"Cerdic is my cousin and marriage between cousins is forbidden by the gods," Ricole pointed out. "And Cerdic already has a wife."

"Cerdic's wife has given him only one child in five years of marriage," Leofgar explained. "He accuses her of having destroyed his unborn children by witchcraft, and desires to put her away and take another wife."

"Then Cerdic is wicked, father, and I would not wish to marry a wicked man," Ricole said firmly.

"You might have no choice, my daughter."

"Then I shall refuse to marry anyone," Ricole said lightly. "I pray you do not concern yourself, father—I promise I will not marry anyone if the matter causes you anxiety."

"You do not understand, Ricole," Leofgar persisted, his voice weak and breathless with the effort of speaking. "I fear for you, for what the future holds for you."

"The future lies with the gods—they will protect me," Ricole said confidently.

She heard the door of the bower open and turned to see Cerdic quietly entering the chamber.

"How is my lord uncle?" Cerdic asked, in a low voice.

Ricole turned back to speak to Leofgar. "Here is Cerdic to see you, my father. He enquires as to your health. Father, why do you stare at me like that? Why. . . ?"

Cerdic leaned forward and felt for Leofgar's pulse.

"He is dead, Ricole," he said sorrowfully. "Our lord is dead."

Ricole said nothing. Her expression serene, her eyes void of tears, she summoned her ladies and slaves to attend the dead chieftain, to lay out his body in the manner prescribed. Leofgar would lie in state, his weapons beside him, until the morrow when he would be placed on a great funeral pyre and ritually cremated.

Having issued her instructions, Ricole turned and left the chieftain's bower and retired to her own bower in the chieftain's wooden dwelling in the palisaded burgh. Her eyes suddenly brimming with tears, she knelt down in front of the small wooden statue of Freya, the goddess of beauty and fertility.

She remained there on her knees for a long time, beseeching Freya for her blessing and protection. She was conscious of an overwhelming sense of loss. She had loved her father devotedly. Having known neither mother, nor brothers and sisters, Leofgar had been all in all to her and he had seen to it that she had been reared, as befitted the daughter of an Anglian lord, in protected innocence.

Despite her brave words to Leofgar, Ricole was well aware of her aloneness, of her danger. How could she, a defenceless woman, control the fierce warriors of her people? She was not wholly oblivious of the feelings she aroused in men. She had recognised the lust in their eyes, the lascivious smiles, the crude meanings behind the honeyed words. She had merely pretended not to understand and had taken shelter behind an air of cool innocence.

Leofgar had at one time considered marrying her to Morcar, a warrior of renown and the leader of Leofgar's *hearth-horde*, his bodyguard, for Leofgar had considered Morcar the man best able to protect her after his death. But Ricole had dissuaded him. Morcar was cruel and merciless, just as Leofgar's elder brother had been. Morcar treated the slaves with brutality and he already had three concubines. Nay, Ricole had not wished to marry Morcar.

I shall marry one day, Ricole said to herself. I am in my sixteenth year and there is no necessity for haste. I shall marry one day, but I shall marry a man chosen by the gods, for the gods surely have a purpose for me. They will show me their purpose in their own good time, will they not?

Conscious of her doubts, her fears, her sudden desolation and vulnerability, Ricole prostrated herself before the statue, and recited aloud and with feverish intensity the litany of Freya:

> "Holy Freya, mother of the gods, pray for me,
> Queen of Heaven, pray for me,
> Queen of peace, pray for me,
> Queen of Angles, pray for me,
> Mother of good counsel, pray for me,
> Mother most powerful, pray for me,
> Mother most merciful, pray for me,
> Mirror of justice, protect me,
> Shrine of the spirit, protect me,
> Mystical rose, protect me,
> Morning star, protect me,
> Cause of our joy, protect me,
> Comfort of those in trouble, protect me."

TWO

Ricole completed her prayers and remained on her knees, her face wet with tears, gazing up at the statue. Despite her tears, she already felt a little more at ease, a little less fearful of the future.

There was a loud rap on the door of her bower.

"Enter," she called absently and not turning round, for she imagined the entrant to be her handmaiden, Ceolburh, who was maybe a trifle hesitant of intruding on her grief.

But the footsteps that entered the bower were booted and masculine and could not be mistaken for Ceolburh's barefooted tread.

"Morcar!" Ricole exclaimed, her heart missing a beat as she turned hastily towards the newcomer. "What brings you to a lady's bower?"

Broad-shouldered and handsome, Morcar's blatant masculinity seemed to dominate the bower. He bowed courteously.

"Necessity, my lady," he said.

"Necessity?"

"Your lord father is dead, alas—you could well be in danger," Morcar answered evenly. "I have just heard the sorrowful news from Cerdic and hastened hither to offer you my condolences and protection."

"Your protection?" Ricole asked, warily.

"Already the warriors cast lots as to which of them shall take you to wife," Morcar explained.

Ricole's face drained of colour. "How dare you come to

me with such wicked lies! You came here to taunt me, Morcar, did you not, for you can surely not be serious?"

"I am telling you the truth, my lady," Morcar assured her earnestly.

"Mother of the gods! How could the warriors act so! My lord father is not yet cold. . . ."

"True!" Morcar agreed, sardonically. "Your lord father is not yet cold, and already the bodies of men grow hot with lust. Regrettable, my lady, but a fact of life, I fear!"

Ricole's cheeks reddened although she pretended not to understand his meaning. "I shall marry no one," she managed to say with firmness. "I promised my lord father on his death-bed that I would marry no one."

"You will marry me, my lady," Morcar retorted with equal firmness.

"You?" Ricole asked scornfully, leaving him in no doubt of her antipathy to him.

"It was your lord father's wish that we should wed but I understand that you persuaded him to postpone the match," Morcar said evenly. "Doubtless you wished then to give all your time and attention to your dying lord. But now your duty is done, my lady—marry me and I swear I will be a worthy recipient of your time and attention."

"You flatter yourself, Morcar!" Ricole said, scathingly. "I refused to marry you because I did not feel for you as I believe a maiden should feel for her prospective bridegroom. I shall marry no one as yet, for I believe that when the gods wish me to marry they will show me a sign."

"The gods! As a maiden should feel for her prospective bridegroom!" exclaimed Morcar mockingly. "You have hearkened to too many childish tales of romance, my lady. A woman weds where her father chooses, and submits willingly to her new lord."

"And you imagine I would submit willingly to you?"

asked Ricole, trying vainly to hide her growing alarm.

Morcar's gaze was hard and merciless. "Willingly or not, you will submit, my lady," he said.

"And if I refuse to marry you?" Ricole enquired, haughtily.

Morcar made no reply for a moment. His gaze flickered over her from head to toe, a lascivious mocking gaze which left her in no doubt of his feelings for her.

He shrugged. "You must remain in your bower this night —the door will be bolted on the outside and I shall place a strong guard there."

"My handmaiden. . . ."

"Will be permitted to enter with food and wine, and to minister to your needs," Morcar told her, making it clear he had already formed a plan. "Then you will remain alone until the morrow. I shall return at daybreak and you shall inform me then of your decision."

"My decision? I have already given you my decision."

"You have made a decision as to whether or not you will marry me," Morcar said urbanely. "But there is yet time for you to change your mind."

"Never!" exclaimed Ricole whole-heartedly.

"If you refuse to marry me, then you will be given to whomsoever wins you in the lottery," Morcar continued. " 'Tis doubtful if the winner could be persuaded to wait for marriage. At this very moment, Cerdic having informed them of our lord's death, the warriors are behaving like wild beasts. Without their overlord, they are exulting in sudden freedom and they gorge their appetites on meat and ale . . ."

"Enough, Morcar!" cried Ricole angrily. "You are cruel to taunt me thus!"

"I can read it in your eyes that you are afraid, that you know I am speaking the truth."

"If it is as you say, what of you, Morcar?" Ricole demanded. "Could you, the leader of my father's *hearth-horde*, leash those wild beasts as he would have done?"

"The ale they drink has been drugged by my orders, my lady. Soon the roisterers will fall into a stupor and will slumber till daybreak. Then it will all start with renewed vigour—always it is so at such times—and no woman, be she maid or matron, will be safe from the orgies that will follow, unless. . . ." Morcar paused tantalisingly.

"Unless?" Ricole prompted, breathlessly.

"Unless I prevent it."

"You believe you could do that?" Ricole asked, doubtfully.

"I know I could do it, given the right incentive," Morcar answered pointedly. "Was I not the leader of your lord father's *hearth-horde*, the protector of his left arm? Accustomed to obeying me, the men will obey me as they will obey no other. Otherwise the law of the forest will prevail throughout the burgh of Angel. It will be every man for himself, lawlessness will triumph, and power will be seized first by one and then by another, until our tribe as such is no more. Surely, my lady, your maidenhead is a small offering to the cause."

"The cause?" Ricole asked, tremulously.

"The future and well-being of our people."

"You see yourself as chieftain?"

"With you as my willing bride, I see myself as chieftain," Morcar acknowledged.

"And without?" Ricole asked, quietly.

"You would go to the man who wins you in the lottery, and maybe I would still become chieftain," Morcar said complacently.

"A man who would drive such a bargain with a defenceless maiden is no fit chieftain for our people," Ricole said angrily.

"Whom would you choose in my stead, my lady?" Morcar demanded, pertinently.

Ricole seemed suddenly to recover her serenity. "You have given me till the morrow, Morcar. By then, 'tis certain the gods will have made plain their will. By the time my lord father's ashes are cold, I shall know where lies my true path."

"But what if the gods remain silent, my lady?" asked Morcar mockingly.

"They would not be so cruel!" Ricole said, confidently. "They will not desert me in my hour of need. They will not be so heartless as to undo all the good work my lord father did, to thwart his dream of a great future for our race."

Morcar's voice was deceptively gentle. "We could build for the future together, my lady. The warriors will obey me as leader of the *hearth-horde* and, with the *hearth-horde* at my command, no one warrior of the tribe can gainsay me. Become my bride, my lady, and bear me sons, Leofgar's grandsons, who in turn will be the leaders of our people."

"You do not deceive me with such talk, Morcar," Ricole said haughtily. "I know of your reputation and that was my reason for refusing to marry you in the first place. You are cruel and heartless. And what of your concubines?"

Morcar smiled. "If my concubines are your chief concern, the only obstacle to our bridal, I can set your mind at rest, my lady. I would give them up without a qualm," he assured her lightly.

"Two of them are with child, I understand."

Morcar shrugged. "Since their existence clearly offends you and is a hindrance to our union, I swear I shall give orders that my concubines be clubbed to death as soon as you promise to become my wife," he said dispassionately.

Shocked by his words, by his lack of concern for those in his power and for his unborn children, Ricole, white to the lips, watched him in stunned silence for a few moments.

"You would do that for my sake?" she whispered then.

"I would do anything to win you, my lady," Morcar said earnestly. "I shall await your decision with the greatest eagerness."

"I can give you my answer now," Ricole said quietly.

"Ah! I thought you would come to your senses, that you would see the advantages of an alliance with me," Morcar said triumphantly.

"My answer is 'nay'," Ricole said defiantly. "Even for the good of our people, and I am not convinced your leadership would be for the good of our people, I could not ally myself to you, Morcar. The gods cannot desire that I marry so unspeakable a villain—they will yet come to my rescue."

Taken aback, Morcar watched her without speaking for a moment, his eyes clearly expressing his fury. For one terrifying moment he stepped towards her and Ricole feared he was about to strike her, or to take her there and then against her will.

But then, "Till daybreak, my lady," he said curtly and, turning abruptly, strode from the chamber.

THREE

Ricole spent a troubled and sleepless night alone in her bower. Grief-stricken by her father's death, and fearful for the future of her people and herself, the thoughts went round and round in her mind, increasing her anxiety and adding to her misery with every passing moment.

The knowledge that her father had considered Morcar the most able warrior to take command and subdue the wild Anglian warriors, only added to Ricole's confusion. Was she right in refusing to make an alliance with Morcar that would strengthen his influence and standing with her people? Were the tales told of him, of his cruelty and ruthlessness, exaggerated? she wondered. Morcar's blatant masculinity was a powerful attraction to women, a fact of which he was doubtless aware, and the tales of his conquests, his seductions, his brutality, were never-ending. He had made no attempt to deny his concubines, and that two of them were with child.

Ricole shrugged. Am I being foolish, a trifle over-sensitive perchance? Am I being selfish in refusing to marry Morcar, in hoping that one day I shall marry a man I love? All men take slaves and concubines. The gods do not forbid it. The law does not forbid it. Whilst fornication with freewomen is forbidden, every Anglian male is permitted to take slaves at will. Slaves, male or female, are the property, the chattels, of their masters and are expected to please their masters in all things.

Why then am I so shocked by the knowledge of Morcar's concubines? she asked herself. It is not the thought of the concubines themselves that disturbs me; it is the remembrance of Morcar's expression as he announced quite lightly his intention of having them killed as soon as I promised to marry him. His face was dispassionate, his voice quiet and without emotion, as if such brutality would cause him not a single qualm. Could I give myself to such a man? Even for the good of my people, could I do so? What if Morcar should tire of me after our marriage? Am I, the daughter of his people's beloved chieftain, merely an adjunct to his ego? Does not he desire to attain the unattainable? Many men desire me. Morcar is aware of that. But if I became Morcar's bride, he alone would possess me. I would become his property, as his slaves are, and—Ricole shuddered—would I in the end fare any better than they? They say his lusts are insatiable. Could I bring myself, even for my people's sake, to marry such a man?

Ricole's anxieties were still unresolved when at daybreak Ceolburh was permitted to enter the bower, bringing her a bowl of buttermilk to drink.

"My lady, Morcar bids me say that he will attend you here in half an hour's time," Ceolburh said, as she gave the buttermilk to Ricole.

"I must be ready to greet him suitably attired," said Ricole.

"Which gown shall I fetch for you, my lady?"

"I shall don my newest gown."

"The red one, my lady?"

"Nay, the black—the seamstresses, I understand, have just finished it."

"Indeed, my lady, but 'tis as yet without embroidery or trimming of any kind," Ceolburh told her. "The seamstresses have been awaiting your instructions."

"I shall wear it just as it is, Ceolburh," Ricole said firmly, finishing the buttermilk and climbing from the bed. "In a gown of plain and unadorned black, I shall be suitably attired as a mourning daughter."

"But, my lady, what of Morcar?" Ceolburh asked, in surprise. "He will be here anon, and as a prospective bride. . . ."

"A prospective bride?" asked Ricole sharply. "Who speaks of my being a prospective bride?"

"Word has got around, my lady . . ." Ceolburh hesitated.

"I pray you continue, Ceolburh."

" 'Tis thought you'll wed Morcar before Earl Leofgar's funeral this evening. They say . . ." Again Ceolburh paused.

"Go on, Ceolburh. What do they say?"

"Well, my lady, there was wild goings-on in the Heorot last night by all accounts and you must have heard sounds of merriment even from here," Ceolburh explained. "My brother told me of it this morning, for all we maidens locked ourselves away in our homesteads for fear we'd find ourselves lacking a maidenhead by morning! My brother says there was drinking and quarrelling, and then some of the leading warriors cast lots as to who should . . . should. . . ."

"Should what, Ceolburh?" prompted Ricole.

"Should marry you, my lady."

"Marry me!" exclaimed Ricole.

"But then, it seems, fighting broke out real serious, and Morcar called the warriors to order. 'I can tell you which of us is to marry the lady Ricole,' he said. 'The lady Ricole has promised to be mine.' There was cries of disbelief at this, my lady, for many, knowing Morcar's reputation and that you'd already refused him in your lord father's lifetime, doubted the truth of what he said. But Morcar wasn't deterred, not he. 'I, Morcar, tell you this,' he said. 'Before the body of our late-lamented lord is given into the embrace of the funeral flames, the lady Ricole will be mine'."

"What happened then, Ceolburh?"

"Cerdic, my brother says, got very angry. He swore to kill Morcar there and then. He drew his sword, crying that none but he should wed you, my lady. 'Am I not my lady's kinsman?' he asked. 'Since she lacks a father, is it not the duty of her kinsmen to protect her from the attentions of ambitious upstarts?'"

"Cerdic fought with Morcar?" Ricole enquired faintly, and clutching at a table for support.

"Nay, your uncles seized Cerdic and dragged him from the Heorot—it seems they feared that in his eagerness he'd be no match for Morcar, and they wished, they said, to have time to discuss the future of the tribe amicably and reasonably with the other elders."

"What happened then?" Ricole asked.

"Morcar called for drinks all round, asking the warriors to drink to his prospective bride, and then there was a bit of a shindy and after that, all of them, says my brother, fell asleep."

"A bit of a shindy?" asked Ricole sharply. "There was more fighting, you mean?"

"I don't rightly know, my lady," Ceolburh said evasively, making Ricole wonder if she knew more than she would admit. "My brother just said there was a bit of a shindy, that's all—he seemed a bit chary of explaining about it. My brother had a thick head this morning and swears the liquor Morcar gave them must have been drugged. Oh, my lady, I'm so fearful for you. Are you truly to wed Morcar?"

"Not if I can help it, Ceolburh," Ricole assured her. "All night I have waited for the gods to show me a sign, to make plain their wishes for me."

"They'll have to be mighty quick then, my lady, for

Morcar will be here anon."

"Go and fetch the black gown, Ceolburh, and help me dress," ordered Ricole.

A quarter of an hour later, when Morcar presented himself at the door of Ricole's bower and curtly dismissed Ceolburh, Ricole was ready to receive him.

Clad in the unadorned black woollen gown, without jewellery or embellishment of any kind, her blonde hair hanging unbound down her back, Ricole greeted Morcar with cool dignity.

Having greeted her formally, Morcar surveyed Ricole for a few moments in silence. He was spellbound by her beauty. Seeking to adopt the severe appearance of a peasant, Ricole had never looked more beautiful. The drab black cloth emphasised the shining glory of her hair, rose and lily rivalled for predominance in her face, and the coral of her lips vied for attention with the blue-green of her eyes. Only the girdle which encircled her slender waist relieved the severe lines of the gown: from it hung none of the customary trinkets worn by women of her race but only, as if in deliberate emphasis, the small but lethal knife which was carried by all freewomen.

"You know why I am here, my lady," Morcar said then, his voice expressionless.

"Nay, since I gave you my answer yesterday, Morcar, I confess I do not know why you are here," Ricole answered coldly.

"I had hoped that having been given time to recover from the shock of your lord father's death, you would see the matter in a different light this morning, my lady."

"Oh, I do, Morcar, I do," Ricole said earnestly.

"Then. . . ."

"Time has but strengthened my determination to marry no one as yet."

"That cannot be."

"You cannot force me to marry you, Morcar, as well you know. I cannot be forced to take my vows before the statue of Freya in the temple," Ricole said coolly.

"True!" Morcar agreed. "No one can force you to make your marriage vows, as you say. But if you persist in your refusal to marry, if you refuse as your father's daughter to make an alliance with me so that together we may maintain law and order amongst our people, there will soon be no law and order. Marriage vows then will mean nothing at all. Each man will fight to take whatsoever or whomsoever he desires and the victor, the most ruthless and unworthy, will take the prize."

"You mean. . . ." Ricole paused, her face paling. She knew there was truth in Morcar's words. If only, she thought, I could be certain that he himself is not the most ruthless and unworthy!

"I mean that together, with you as my bride, we could maintain law and order," Morcar explained. "You really have no alternative, my lady. Should you refuse me, and ignore the needs of our people, you will be taken by force of arms anyway."

"You would let that happen?" Ricole asked, aghast.

"I should make sure it happened," Morcar assured her. "Would not I be the victor? No man can vanquish me in fair combat."

"What of my cousin, Cerdic?" Ricole asked. "He will protect me, as will my other kinsmen."

"They have done little to protect you so far, my lady, or has that little fact escaped your notice?" Morcar asked, tauntingly. "You have virtually been my prisoner here since last night. Cerdic could well present a problem it is true. He is a doughty warrior but in the unlikely event of his vanquishing me, he would have his own axe to grind."

"His own axe? I fail to understand," Ricole admitted.

"You would then be his, body and soul, make no mistake about that, my lady."

"Cerdic is my cousin," Ricole reminded him.

"He is, as you say, your cousin, and he lusts after you. For many moons past he has been casting covetous eyes upon you." Morcar saw, with satisfaction, her involuntary shudder and smiled knowingly. "Of course if you wish to wed Cerdic. . . ."

"I do not," Ricole said emphatically. "I will wed no one."

Morcar sighed ostentatiously. "You weary me with your obstinacy, my lady. Where is your sense of duty? Do you not see the service you will be doing our people if you marry me?"

"What advantage will it be to our people to have a murderous lecher for a chieftain?" Ricole asked, spiritedly. "A man who can state without a qualm that he would murder his unborn children."

Morcar looked at her in surprise. "Unborn children? What do you mean, my lady? Oh, you refer to my concubines and the fact that two of them were in spawn."

"Were?" asked Ricole suspiciously.

"They are dead, my lady, so the thought of them need no longer trouble you."

"Dead? Your concubines? All three?"

"Nay, only the two who were in spawn. The other one yet lives—did I not need consolation last night after your cruel rejection of me?"

"How did they die, Morcar?"

"The warriors became restive last night in the Heorot, as you must have realised, for their wild exuberance could be heard all over the burgh I am told. Desirous of preserving law and order at least until I had learned of your decision this morning, I advised all homesteaders to keep their wives

and daughters and female slaves safely indoors. The warriors quickly became drunk and many fell into a stupor,
may the gods be praised, before they lost control. When
the remainder started to become violent and showed signs
of breaking out of the Heorot and going on a rampage
through the burgh and the surrounding homesteads, I put
my plan into operation."

"What plan?"

"I made two of my concubines dress themselves in their
finery and jewels—I am a generous master, my lady—and
then I took them to the Heorot. 'They are yours,' I said to
the warriors."

"Mother of the gods!" Ricole breathed, in horror.

"That did the trick!" Morcar went on, thankfully. "The
concubines were received with enthusiasm and by the time
they had served my purpose, the drugged mead had taken
effect."

"And the women? What of them?"

"Need you ask? Dead as mutton of course!" Morcar
shrugged carelessly. "There were probably a hundred men
there still sober enough to tumble a wench."

"All those men, and two helpless women who were
already with child," Ricole said, white-faced with shock.
"May the gods forgive you, Morcar, for I fear I never can!"

"Spare me the histrionics!" Morcar exclaimed, impatiently. "As with all women, your judgement is affected
by your emotions. Therein lies your weakness. Only men
recognise the need to sacrifice the lesser to the greater, only
the male is truly objective—hence our superiority. That
explains the basic difference between us, barring a few
pleasurable biological differences of course!"

"Superiority?" Ricole asked, scathingly. "I see no evidence of superiority in upwards of a hundred brave warriors
ravishing to death two helpless women!"

"Fie, my lady! Such melodramatics!" taunted Morcar. "Believe me, the women did not survive the first ten."

"How do you know. . . ?" Ricole started to say, but then she stared at him aghast. "You mean you remained there? You watched?"

"They were sacrificed to a good cause," Morcar said piously, ignoring the question. "They were sacrificed for the well-being of our tribe. You could well learn from such a sacrifice, my lady. You must set aside your own petty scruples and act for the good of our people."

"Marry you, you mean? Never!"

Morcar advanced menacingly towards her. "You are refusing me?"

"I have already refused you," Ricole said, her eyes never leaving his face as her fingers tightened on her knife and she drew it from its sheath. "Come no nearer, Morcar, or I shall use my knife!"

Morcar laughed uproariously. "Such provocation! You tempt me beyond endurance—almost. But I will bide my time till nightfall. You might yet change your mind. I shall arrange a bridal ceremony to take place one hour before your lord father's cremation. Should you persist in your refusal to become my bride, I shall return here after the funeral and have my way with you. Given a few hours alone with you, my lady, 'tis certain I could tame you sufficiently to have won myself a willing bride by morning."

"Never!"

"We shall see! Another day of isolation here, might yet persuade you of your duty."

"As you say, we shall see," retorted Ricole. "Come to my bower this evening with evil intent and you will see only a lifeless corpse awaiting you."

"Idle words! Idle threats! It shows the measure of my regard for you that I do not whip you raw for such obstinacy, my lady. I confess you tempt me grievously. You tempt me not to wait until tonight. But I shall keep my word."

As Morcar turned and strode from the bower, Ricole stood watching till the door closed behind him and she heard him giving curt orders to the guards outside. Then, as soon as she judged him out of earshot, she flung herself on her bed and broke into a storm of weeping.

She was trapped, it seemed, trapped by a brutal and lecherous monster who was already well on the way to becoming the new chieftain. Why do the gods not hearken to my pleas? she asked herself. Why have they turned their backs on my people in their extremity? What sort of future will there be for any of us under the chieftainship of such a man? What can I do? Should I marry Morcar? If I did so, in sacrificing my own freedom and hopes of happiness, would I be able to influence him and intercede for the welfare of our people? Is that what the gods are asking of me? If I tried to love Morcar and to please him, could I perchance influence him for good, turn him from the path of evil? Or would he use me as long as I pleased him and then, when the novelty of marrying Earl Leofgar's daughter had worn off, dispose of me in much the same way as he did his concubines?

Ricole lay back on her bed, trying desperately to control her weeping, to bring some order to her confused mind. It was nearing the ninth hour of the morning and a whole day of isolation and uncertainty lay ahead of her. She clasped her hands together and started to pray:

"Allfather, oldest of the gods and first guardian of my people, second lord of Armies, third lord of the Spear, fourth Smiter, fifth All-knowing, sixth Fulfiller-of-wishes, seventh Farspoken, eighth Shaker, ninth Burner, tenth Destroyer, eleventh Protector, and twelfth Gelding, help me in my extremity. Make plain your will, O Mighty One, that I may do whatsoever is in the best interests of my people, and I beseech you to prevail upon the other gods to come to my aid. . . ."

FOUR

The day that followed Leofgar's death was the first day of *Thrimilci*,[1] the first day of the Northern Spring in the 5469th year[2] since the beginning of the world.

As it neared the ninth hour of the morning, two fishermen mending their nets on the shore of Angel, that desolate windswept shore of an estuary off the eastern coast of Denmark, looked up in alarm at the sudden darkening of the sky.

"Looks as if there's a storm brewing, Anlaf," said one. "Who'd have thought it? 'Twas bright sunshine a few minutes ago, a real spring day."

"A storm—that's all we need!" exclaimed Anlaf gloomily. "With Earl Leofgar dead, the outlook's bleak enough as it is. Who's going to take his place? That's what I'd like to know? Who's to keep the warriors in check and protect us and our womenfolk? Who's to guard us and our families from attacks by other tribes? Freya protect us, it's growing black as night!"

"There's something mighty strange about that there sky, mate. Look up there!"

"By Frigg! There are stars shining up there in the heavens. It's dark as night, there's no sign of a storm, and it's nearing the ninth hour of the morning on the first day of spring! I don't like it at all, Sidroc."

[1] Month of May when the cows were milked thrice daily.
[2] A.D. 280. Pagan Angles believed that the world began 5189 B.C.

"No more do I. Coming so soon after Earl Leofgar's death, 'tis surely an ill-omen for our people."

"And that's not all, Sidroc. Look yonder in the sky!"

"Frigg protect us! It must be the star comet of which the wisemen and the priests have spoken. 'Tis like a ball of fire, a spinning, twisting ball of fire."

The fishermen gaped, open-mouthed and fearful, at the curious phenomenon, at the whirling mass that looked in its dazzling brilliance like a fast-moving sun in a night sky. But there was no sun. There was no light. Utter darkness had descended upon the daytime earth. Sidroc and Anlaf could no longer see each other: all they could see was the ball of fire.

The disc-like object seemed to be falling towards the earth, spinning at breathtaking speed towards the shore of Angel. Calling on the gods for protection, the fishermen clutched at each other in the darkness, seeking for both divine assistance and human comfort in their terror of the unknown.

Just before the ball of fire reached the earth, the sky suddenly began to lighten until, in a few seconds and just as the ninth hour was reached, the world around them reappeared and the familiar shore of Angel was again bathed in bright spring sunlight.

"Thought it was the end of the world, Anlaf," said Sidroc shakily.

"Me too," Anlaf agreed. "I thought our last hour had come."

"You're an optimist, mate! Last hour indeed! Last second, I thought! Funny isn't it, everything looks the same as usual now, as if we imagined the whole thing. The sea's calm, unusually calm, and the sun's giving off a lot of heat for the time of year."

"What's that, Sidroc?"

"What's what?"

"Out there in the sea. Looks like a boat—one of the fishing boats must 'ave slipped its moorings in the night.

"Nay, take another look, Anlaf. It isn't one of our boats —it's much too big."

"An invasion vessel perchance?" asked Anlaf in sudden alarm.

"Nay, there's no oarsmen. I can see that from here and there's no sail neither. It must have been beset by a storm and lost all hands overboard, and now it's drifting in on the incoming tide."

"Incoming tide! And you call yourself a fisherman, Sidroc! Shame on ye! That there's an outgoing tide."

"Then the wind must have. . . ."

"The wind is westerly," Anlaf pointed out.

"No oarsmen, and a contrary wind and tide!" exclaimed Sidroc in astonishment. "What manner of vessel is it then? One of us had best go up to the burgh and tell our lord."

"Earl Leofgar is dead, remember."

"Freya protect us, I had forgotten for the moment," Sidroc admitted. "The sight of that comet's unnerved me, I don't mind admitting it, and pushed other matters right out of my mind."

"One of us had best go and tell the elders of our people . . ."

"Them's no use. The warriors was rampaging, sodden with drink, half the night. Didn't ye hear them, Anlaf? The elders could do nothing with them by all accounts. Only Morcar can control the warriors."

"Then one of us must go and tell Morcar," Anlaf said. "He was leader of our lord's *hearth-horde*—he'll know what to do. Could be that some hostile neighbouring tribe's heard of Earl Leofgar's death and seeks to take our people by surprise."

B

"There's no need for us to trouble ourselves, mate," Sidroc said, pointing towards the pathway which led down the slope from the burgh. "Look, someone else must have raised the alarm, for Morcar and many of our people are hastening to the shore."

The two men watched intently as the mysterious vessel drifted towards them. It moved slowly but with uncanny precision and direction as if motivated by an unseen hand. There was still no sign of life aboard. Or was there?

On the ship's prow perched a large black raven. Resembling a figurehead, it remained dignified and motionless as if it alone controlled the ship, as if it were both oarsman and helmsman.

Anlaf chuckled. "Welcome to the shore of Angel, Sir Raven," he said with a mocking obeisance.

Sidroc stared at the ship in silence. Seeing it clearly for the first time, he was astonished by its size. His experienced eye judged it to be about eighty feet long from fore to aft and sixteen feet broad. Mastless and clinker-built, it had rowlocks for sixteen oars down each side, and the gunwale was fitted with shields which were painted alternately yellow and black.

All the inhabitants of Angel had witnessed and been disturbed by the strange phenomenon, by the total eclipse of the sun and the ball of fire. Drawn to the shore by the news—delivered breathlessly to the burgh by another fisherman—of a mysterious ship, many people were now gathering on the shore.

There were exclamations of astonishment, of disbelief, and of superstitious invocation to the gods by the more timorous, as the ship journeyed purposefully towards the jetty and it became clear that it was propelled wholly without human agency.

As it reached shallow water, men waded excitedly out to

seize it and moor it to the jetty, eager to discover its secret.

As soon as the ropes had been made fast, the men from the shore peered inside the ship. The sight which met their gaze did nothing to satisfy their curiosity or allay their fears.

The man who was lying, apparently dead, in the bottom of the ship, was dressed in a leather tunic and breeches. His head was encased in a silver helmet which shone brightly in the sunlight, a helmet whose front panel appeared to be made of glass through which his face, his eyes closed, could plainly be seen.

"Our visitor is curiously apparelled—clearly he comes from a tribe unknown to us," said Morcar with a complacency he was far from feeling. He turned to speak to two warriors of the *hearth-horde*. "Go aboard and ascertain what caused his death—I can see no obvious sign of injury."

The men hesitated. "The raven, sir," one of them said.

"The raven? Blood of Tiw! You fear a raven, Oswy?" Morcar asked, derisively.

"It looks menacing, sir."

"Ravens always look menacing, my friend," Morcar said trenchantly. "You, a warrior of the *hearth-horde* admit to being afraid of a raven? You shall be the first to investigate —go to it, Oswy."

All this time the raven had remained motionless. Still perched in dignified disdain upon the prow, it showed no more sign of life than the inert figure in the bottom of the ship. Only its hooded eyes, brooding and predatory, showed it to be more than a mere figurehead.

Goaded by the derisory taunts of his comrades, Oswy reluctantly started to climb over the side of the ship. At once, the raven sprang into life. Its wings spanned out and it flew at Oswy, batting him ferociously with its wings until, forced to relinquish his hold on the ship's side, he fell back painfully upon the jetty.

"Our friend, Oswy, the great warrior, has been given the bird!" Morcar chortled, joining in the laughter of his men. "Let us see if you can do better, Ulf."

Ulf shook his head emphatically, his fear of the occult powers greater than his fear of his leader.

"Nay, sir, with respect, there are evil forces at work here, 'tis clear," he said. "I'll take my chance of a flogging for disobeying orders but I'll not board that ship of my own free will."

Exasperated by Ulf's obstinacy and fearful, in the present state of unrest in the tribe, of losing control of his men, Morcar cursed roundly, smote Ulf a heavy blow which knocked him backward into the water, and himself strode to the side of the jetty and climbed aboard.

Morcar heard rather than saw the powerful wings that flew swiftly towards him, he felt rather than saw the cruel beak that pierced his right eye. He heard his own involuntary scream of pain and saw with his remaining eye the blood that poured from his eye socket on to his tunic. Shielding his remaining eye with his hands, he ordered his men to assist him from the ship.

" 'Tis a nasty wound, sir," Oswy said, the merest hint of triumph in his voice. "The lady Ricole is said to be greatly skilled in healing. Shall I take you to her?"

"Nay, bid the lady Ricole tend me here," Morcar said, gritting his teeth against the pain. "Tell her to bring bandages and medicaments. Once she has stanched the wound, the ship must be boarded."

"But what of the raven, sir?" asked another of the warriors uneasily, as Oswy went in search of Ricole.

"I, Morcar, shall kill the raven."

Ricole, released from her bower, showed no sign of her anxieties as she walked, graceful and serene, a hooded cloak covering the plain black gown, over the sandy shore and down to the water's edge.

"I hear you are grievously wounded, Morcar," she said compassionately. "I pray you return with me to the burgh where the wound can be suitably tended."

"Do the best you can here, my lady, for I have work to do," said Morcar grimly.

"Work to do? With such a wound, Morcar?" Ricole enquired disapprovingly, glancing down into the boat. "And is that not another wounded man? Your adversary perchance?"

"My adversary is perched on the prow, my lady, lord of all he surveys," Morcar answered. "My lord raven has yet to answer to my sword."

"The man is dead? How came he here, Morcar? And in such strange apparel?" Ricole asked lightly, as if the matter were of little consequence to her.

"You might well ask, my lady," Morcar said. "How came he here indeed? We would all like an answer to that question."

"Now, Morcar, sit down there on the sand whilst I tend your wound," Ricole said then, her voice cool and practical. "Keep quite still whilst I cleanse it. You have lost your eye, alas, but the wound will soon heal with the aid of this medicament. There! Now I will place a pad over your eye socket, so, and then I will bandage it to keep the pad in place."

Ricole worked deftly and skilfully, and then, just as quickly and skilfully, as if all her life she had commanded her father's *hearth-horde*, she issued an order to the warriors.

"Seize him!" she cried sharply.

Galvanised into action by the tone of command, several

warriors leapt forward and seized the now-protesting Morcar.

"Blood of Tiw!" Morcar cried, furiously. "Let me go, you bastards!"

"Be at peace, Morcar," Ricole said sweetly. "You are a wounded man. You are a little feverish. You must rest awhile."

"I need no rest, my lady—why are you treating me thus?" Morcar demanded, angrily.

"I wish to discover what ails the man in the ship."

"He is dead."

"But how came he here dead?" Ricole asked, with a puzzled frown. "He is not a putrefying corpse. His hands look warm and life-like. I must see what ails him."

"I beg you for your own safety not to touch him, my lady," Morcar said pleadingly. "Do not attempt to board the ship or the raven will attack you as it did me."

Ricole smiled ruefully. "Perchance that would solve all my problems, Morcar. Perchance a one-eyed maiden would hold less appeal for lustful men."

"My lady, I beg you. . . ."

"You show concern that I too might lose an eye?" Ricole interrupted, mockingly. "Fie, Morcar! If I married you, perchance we could then breed a race of one-eyed monsters."

"It ill-becomes a maiden to speak so," Morcar said disapprovingly, and turned to his captors. "For Tiw's sake, stop her! She is your lord's daughter—it is your duty to protect her from danger."

Overawed by the determined light in Ricole's eyes, and restrained by Morcar's unwise reminder that she was their beloved and recently-dead chieftain's daughter, the men gave no heed to Morcar's appeal.

All watched uneasily and with bated breath as Ricole, aided by two of her women who had attended her to the shore, climbed gracefully over the side of the ship. There were gasps of horror and cries of warning, as the raven spread its wings wide and swooped from its perch.

But the onlookers soon fell silent, their attention riveted by what followed. The raven circled the ship nine times and then, cawing loudly, it alighted upon the inert body of the man.

Ricole ignored the raven.

She walked steadily over to the man and, kneeling down by his side, felt for his pulse.

"It is as I thought," she murmured to herself. "He still breathes."

"Caw! Caw!" agreed the hoarse voice of the raven.

Ricole unbuckled the complicated straps which held the shining helmet in place and lifted it gently from the unconscious man.

She gazed at him for a few moments, her mind arrested by his beauty. Then, with soft, sensitive hands, she examined his head and neck for signs of injury.

"I can find nothing wrong, my lord raven," she said absently. "Your master sleeps fast methinks."

"Caw! Caw!" agreed the raven.

Even as Ricole watched, the stranger opened his eyes, eyes that were vividly green and beautiful. He looked about himself wonderingly, as if trying to muster his wits and discover where he was. Then his gaze focused on Ricole.

"Who are you?" he asked in the Anglian tongue, his voice pleasing and well-modulated.

"I am Ricole, daughter of the late Earl Leofgar, lord of Angel."

"Of course, my lady. Forgive me, I should have realised," the stranger said.

"And you, sir? Who are you?" Ricole asked.

"I am Woden, lord of the raven."

"You are from Schleswig, sir? Or from Frisia perchance?"

The stranger looked puzzled. "I am Woden, lord of the raven," he said again.

"Whence do you come, Woden, lord of the raven?"

"I cannot remember. I traversed many seas. There was much darkness and a ball of fire. I was a ball of fire. . . ." Woden's voice tailed off into silence.

"We at Angel saw the ball of fire, my lord," Ricole said. "Perchance it killed your comrades here in the ship and stunned you. Perchance it struck you senseless and you are the only survivor. Indeed that must be the answer. Be at peace, lord of the raven. I will summon men to bear you up to the burgh, where we will take care of you till you are restored to health and your memory has returned."

She stood up and beckoned to a group of men who were regarding her now with respect not unmixed with awe. They came forward at her signal, but eyed the raven warily.

"My people fear the raven, my lord," Ricole said.

"The raven will not molest them whilst I am in control," Woden explained. "He is called Huginn and is my protector. He guards me when I sleep and, even then, attacks only those who would harm me."

"Can a dumb creature such as a raven distinguish between friend and enemy?" Ricole asked, doubtfully.

Woden smiled. "I cannot answer for all ravens, but Huginn has powers beyond the reach of most. He takes his power from me when I sleep."

Woden stretched himself as if his muscles were a little cramped, and then slowly got to his feet. He was about six-feet-six-inches tall, broad of shoulder and vigorously made, Ricole saw, and he stood steady as a rock, showing no signs of injury or illness. He courteously refused the warriors' hands that reached out to assist him disembark, and then turned to Ricole.

"Allow me, my lady," he said gravely and then, lifting her with ease, he carried her over the side of the ship and placed her gently on the jetty.

Then he turned again to the ship. Ricole watched him curiously, sensing his apparent reluctance to leave it for the hospitality of an unknown shore and people. It was as if the ship were a haven, Ricole thought, a last link with the place whence he had come.

"I would beg one favour of you, my lady," he said to Ricole. "I ask that my ship be stowed away just as it is, in one of your winter boat-houses."

Ricole and the warriors followed the direction of his gaze, seeing the curious and unfamiliar objects in the ship. From the outside, though large and unmanned, it had looked normal enough. But inside, on panels fixed below the customary wall of shields, were wires and tubes, dials and strange numerals.

"You are our guest, Woden, lord of the raven," Ricole said, stifling her curiosity. "We gladly accede to your request."

FIVE

It seemed to Ricole as, accompanied by her women and surrounded by a chattering, excited throng, she escorted her
guest back to the burgh, that the gods had not after all
turned a deaf ear to her pleas.

She had been released, for the time being, from captivity;
Morcar's influence had been weakened by her own prompt
action in giving him into temporary custody of the warriors; and it was plain that her people saw the mysterious
arrival of this handsome stranger as a good omen, a sign
that the gods had not forsaken them in their need.

Released from the warriors' hold and in considerable pain,
Morcar had quickly retired from the scene to nurse his
wound and give thought to his next move. Despite his fury
at the unlooked-for development, nothing had changed for
Morcar except his appearance. For the loss of his eye and
the consequent marring of his handsome features, he placed
the blame squarely on the stranger. Even before he had regained consciousness, the lord of the raven had shown himself to be Morcar's enemy. But Morcar must bide his time.
He must make new plans. After the funeral tonight, he
would find a way of disposing of his enemy, and Ricole
and the chieftainship would yet be his.

As befitted an honoured guest and in accordance with
Ricole's instructions, Woden was accommodated in a bower
in the chieftain's dwelling. On arrival there, he graciously
declined offers of food and drink, but displayed a marked

disposition for slumber.

"You are weary, my lord?" Ricole enquired as, accompanied by her handmaidens, she visited him in his bower.

"My journey was long, and covering many thousands of miles in so short a time. . . ." Woden's voice tailed off into silence as if he were unsure how best to express himself.

"How short a time, my lord?" Ricole asked, curiously.

"I cannot answer you with certainty, my lady, but a very short time methinks. Not more than an hour perchance," Woden answered vaguely. "I need time to adapt to my new surroundings, to become acclimatised. Forgive me, my lady, but if I might be permitted to slumber for a while, I shall then be as good as new."

Ricole smiled indulgently. " 'Tis clear, my lord, you are still a little light-headed from your ordeal. You were beset by a storm, your companions were washed overboard, and doubtless a blow on the head robbed you for a time of your memory. You are still a little confused, as is only to be expected. Many thousands of miles indeed! And in not more than an hour! We shall leave you now to sleep off the effects of your ordeal."

"I am grateful, my lady, for your understanding."

"My lord father's funeral will take place at dusk in the Sacred Grove," Ricole explained. "Afterwards a feast will be set out in the Heorot. With your permission, my lord, I will have my servants awaken you then, for it would please my people to have you honour us with your presence at the feast. There is much unrest amongst my people at the present time. Already the Witenagemot has met to elect a new chieftain as is customary before the cremation of a departed chieftain, but they have failed to reach agreement. All fear Morcar. . . ."

"Morcar?" Woden asked.

"He whose eye was stolen by your raven, my lord."

"So I already have an enemy among your people," Woden said quietly, as if to himself. "Know yourself and know your enemy—those are the first precepts of knowledge."

"Now that Morcar is incapacitated, my cousin Cerdic seeks to assume Morcar's authority with the warriors." Ricole sighed. "Alas, my lord, we are in dire need of guidance."

Woden made no reply. Woden was fast asleep. He had fallen back upon the couch and was sleeping as peacefully as an infant.

Smiling gently, Ricole beckoned to her handmaidens and stepped lightly from the chamber.

*   *   *

As dusk fell on that May evening, Ricole stood beside the elders of her people, and gazed for the last time upon her father's face.

The great funeral pyre had been set up in the Sacred Grove, a large clearing in the forest a quarter of a mile from the burgh, and where the temple of Freya stood. Logs and kindling had been piled around Earl Leofgar's body, and the dead chieftain's shield and helmet had been placed beside him.

Ricole tenderly kissed the stone-cold lips of her father and then, accompanied by her women, she returned to the burgh, to weep in the privacy of her bower whilst the funeral, at which no women were present, took place.

As soon as Ricole had departed, the warriors gathered in a great circle around the funeral pyre, and Leofgar's brother, Siferth, his closest kinsman, stepped forward. Taking a burning brand, Siferth thrust the brand amongst the kindling and, as the first giant flame leapt upward into the darkness, two loud cries issued forth as with one voice from the throats of the encircling warriors:

"Leof . . . g . . . ar! Leof . . . g . . . ar!"

The cries echoed and re-echoed around the Sacred Grove, seeming to merge with the flames which were now leaping high into the air, and then receded slowly as if losing themselves in the surrounding forest.

The cries were those of a people bidding farewell to a great and honoured chieftain, a man who had ruled them with wisdom and justice, with compassion and strength. They were the cries of a people who felt themselves forsaken, who feared for the future, who lacked a leader to replace the beloved chieftain they had lost.

* * *

The burgh of Angel, situated between the shores of the estuary and the great forest, was a large palisaded village in which Leofgar had dwelt with his family, his thanes, his servants and his slaves, numbering in all about five hundred inhabitants. The thanes, the tribal warriors, were headed by the *housecarles*, the picked men, led by Morcar, who had formed Leofgar's *hearth-horde*.

The central feature of the burgh was the Heorot, the lofty gabled mead-hall, one hundred feet long, where the warriors ate and slept. Its wooden walls were hung with tapestries, and along the centre of its rush-strewn floor was a sunken hearth from which the smoke escaped through a hole in the roof.

When, after the funeral, the warriors and chief persons of the tribe took their places in the Heorot for the feast which was to follow, the chieftain's bench seat, customarily placed at the further end of the Heorot, was conspicuously empty. Despite this fact and the pain of his wound, Morcar had taken his customary place as leader of Leofgar's *hearth-*

horde, on the left of the empty chair. Ricole was seated on the right of the empty chair, and Woden, the honoured guest, was seated beside her.

Such a feast was a sober occasion, a funeral repast which was customarily partaken in silence. Despite the muted voices and conversations which were in striking contrast to the noisy merriment that usually accompanied a feast, Ricole was conscious of the tension around her.

She sensed the restlessness of Morcar who had already made plain his enmity towards Woden; of her cousin Cerdic who, since Morcar's declaration of his intention of marrying Ricole, kept a baleful watch on Morcar, seeking an opportunity to dispose of his rival; of her uncles and other cousins who each sought the chieftainship for themselves or their offspring. All were disturbed by the arrival of the handsome stranger who sat at her right-hand, the man from the sea who had appeared so mysteriously among them and seemed already to have won himself an honoured place.

Ricole observed the eyes of the warriors on Woden. They were watching him interestedly and questioningly, with undisguised curiosity not unmixed with awe and admiration. Who is he? they were asking themselves. He bears no sign of injury or illness. He is tall and vigorously made and god-like, and moves with a lithe and noble grace which sets him apart from the members of Earl Leofgar's family.

"You slept well, my lord?" Ricole enquired softly, of Woden.

"I did indeed, my lady."

"One of my uncles suggested you might have wished to attend the funeral rites, but I gave orders that you were not to be disturbed—the funeral would have held no meaning for you, since my lord father was unknown to you," Ricole said gently.

"I was there, my lady," Woden said matter-of-factly.

"You were!" exclaimed Ricole. "No one told me you were there."

"No one saw me, I think," Woden explained. " I watched from the edge of the forest. I had no wish to intrude."

"My people would have welcomed your presence, my lord," Ricole assured him. "But of what interest was the funeral of an unknown chieftain to you?"

"I have met Earl Leofgar's daughter—that was commendation enough, my lady."

Ricole overheard Morcar's murmured disapproval of Woden's compliment. Morcar makes plain his resentment and hatred of Woden, she thought to herself. Perchance that is understandable. Was it not Woden's raven that robbed him of his eye?

So the lord of the raven seeks to ingratiate himself with the lady Ricole, does he? Morcar was thinking to himself. Not satisfied with robbing me of an eye, with thwarting my plan for keeping the lady Ricole captive until she promised to be mine, he now sets himself up as my rival. The lady Ricole is beautiful and desirable. But the lady Ricole, like all women, has little brain. She does not recognise the danger of placing a stranger, an unknown man who arrived upon our shore under mighty suspicious circumstances, at her right hand. Perchance he has been sent here by an enemy tribe, to espy the situation here at Angel, to win the lady Ricole's confidence and make himself her husband and our chieftain.

Having reached this alarming conclusion, Morcar's hand went instinctively to his sword hilt, a gesture not unnoticed by Ricole. Her heart-beats quickened with anxiety. Is Morcar about to create a scene, to challenge our guest to a fight? Nay, she told herself firmly, even Morcar would not so far flout the Anglian laws of hospitality as to attack an unarmed man who has taken salt with him. But once outside in the darkness—what then? I must warn Woden of his danger, intimate that all here are not kindly disposed towards him.

"I see you are unarmed, my lord," she said softly. " 'Twas not wise of you to attend my father's funeral unarmed. Since the death of my lord father, my people are restless and uneasy. Having no leader as yet, they fear treachery."

"Unarmed, you say, my lady?" Woden smiled and looked pointedly towards Huginn, who was perched as motionless as a taxidermist's model on the back of his chair. "Nay, I am far from unarmed."

Recalling the bloody mess that had once been Morcar's right eye, Ricole shuddered.

"Have you no weapons, my lord?" she asked.

Woden nodded. "My sword and spear are still in the ship."

"And your shield and battle-axe?" Ricole asked, curiously. "Are they in the ship also?"

"I possess neither shield nor battle-axe."

Ricole concealed her surprise. "Give me leave, my lord, and I will send servants to fetch your sword and spear."

"Nay, my lady, none but I must touch the contents of the ship," Woden said with firm emphasis, as if the matter were all-important. "I shall collect them myself at the appropriate time."

"As you will, my lord," Ricole said a little coldly, feeling she had been rebuffed. "But lacking sword and spear, I urge you to have a care for your own safety."

"You are concerned for my welfare, my lady?" Woden asked quietly, his disturbingly direct gaze meeting hers.

Flushing slightly, Ricole looked demurely down at the table, her long lashes veiling her eyes from his scrutiny.

"You are the guest of my people, my lord," she said a trifle haughtily. "As such, your welfare concerns me."

"I am deeply grateful, my lady," Woden said gravely.

SIX

Ricole was the first to leave the Heorot after the banquet, as befitted the sorrowing daughter of a dead chieftain. She returned to the chieftain's dwelling which had been her home during all of her sixteen years and, dismissing her handmaidens, seated herself disconsolately in the rocking chair in front of the blazing log fire in the living chamber.

The funeral over, she knew that the next few days, or even hours, would see a crisis in the affairs of her people. Since the Witenagemot had met and the Witan, the tribal councillors, had failed to reach unanimity in electing a new chieftain, the way was open for the most powerful and ruthless of the warriors to take the law into his own hands. Without an obvious leader, since Leofgar had left no heir, the chieftainship would fall to the man most able to influence the warriors. In such an event, the Witan would be powerless.

She was equally aware that whoever became chieftain, whether by fair means or foul, would take her as his bride in order to strengthen his position with the tribe. Despite the temporary setback to his schemes, Morcar seemed the most likely candidate for chieftainship, but Cerdic and other members of Leofgar's family would certainly not relinquish the leadership lightly.

Ricole rocked herself abstractedly to and fro as if seeking to soothe her troubled mind. Sixteen years of protected security as Leofgar's beloved only child, had left her ill-equipped to cope single-handed with such a situation as had now arisen. To whom could she turn for protection and guidance? Her kinsmen? Each had his own axe to grind. To her kinsmen she was a mere pawn in the contest for the leadership of her people. Until Leofgar's death, Ricole's life had been happy and untroubled. Marriage had always been her destiny, as well she knew, but marriage to a nobleman of her father's choosing, to a chieftain's son of one of the other Anglian tribes. Such an alliance would have brought greater prosperity and security to both their tribes. Love and personal feelings played no part in such an arrangement.

Love? What is love? Ricole asked herself thoughtfully. Ceolburh sometimes speaks of love. She is betrothed to the churl Olaf and is to marry him in a few weeks' time. She goes dreamy-eyed whenever she speaks his name and she clearly longs to become his wife and bear his children. Why? As the wife of a churl who rarely leaves his homestead, she can look forward to nothing more than a lifetime of hard work and child-bearing. She will go to live in a timber-built cottage on the edge of the forest, a cottage where the family will live and sleep in one room, with the cows and pigs housed in a partitioned-off area at one end. And yet Ceolburh yearns for such a life, for Ceolburh loves Olaf.

Ricole sighed. Clearly I have much to learn, since I do not understand Ceolburh's feelings. Love is surely a gentle emotion, a warm feeling of affection, of consideration for the well-being of the beloved. Love is surely what I felt for my father. And yet I would not have gone all dreamy-eyed at the prospect of living with my father in a one-roomed dwelling on the edge of the forest. I know of no man with whom I would wish to live thus. Morcar terrifies me, if the truth be told, and my cousins are selfish and

quarrelsome, and marriage with one's cousin is forbidden
by the gods. Occasionally, men from other tribes visited my
father, but I never conversed with them beyond the rigid
requirements of formality and etiquette. I fear there is no
man for whose embrace I yearn as does Ceolburh for Olaf's
embrace, no man with whom I would wish to bed, whose
children I would wish to bear. There is no man, alas, with
whom I would choose to spend the rest of my life. . . .

Ricole suddenly ceased rocking and gazed pensively into
the fire. Perchance. . . . Nay, that is nonsense! There is *no*
man for whose embrace I yearn as does Ceolburh for Olaf's
embrace, she told herself again, who could bring that glow
to *my* cheek and that brightness to *my* eye. There is no
man with whom I would wish to bed. . . .

"Nay," Ricole said aloud to the empty chamber, "I am
being foolish and imaginative. How could I possibly feel
like that about a man I have only just met, a stranger
about whom I know nothing? I am affected by my aloneness, by the death of my father and my fear for the future."

But I recall how I felt when Woden looked at me, she
thought, when he was sitting beside me in the Heorot and
I begged him to have a care for his safety. His eyes were
kind and gentle, a little amused by my concern for him.
All the same, his gaze disturbed me strangely. Perchance,
after all, if I am truthful, though I would not admit it to
a living soul, there is a man for whose embrace I yearn. . . .

It was at that instant that Ceolburh, her face pale with
concern, quickly came into the chamber.

"My lady, they've taken him!" she cried breathlessly.

"Who has taken whom?" asked Ricole sharply, her heart
missing a beat for already she guessed the answer.

"Morcar and the *hearth-horde* have taken the lord of the
raven, my lady," Ceolburh explained. "Olaf saw it happen
and came to tell me—he said I must tell you at once."

"The lord Woden is unarmed," Ricole said as if to herself, but then she again addressed Ceolburh. "What of the raven?"

"It seems that Morcar and the *hearth-horde* surrounded and captured the stranger when he left the Heorot after the feast, and that the raven flew away, my lady."

"Where have they taken the lord Woden?" Ricole asked, white-faced with anxiety.

"They've taken him to the Sacred Grove, Olaf says, and they've chained him to the post outside the temple."

"Fetch me my cloak, Ceolburh," Ricole ordered. "I shall go at once to the Sacred Grove."

"My lady, I beg you consider the danger of going there alone at such a late hour," Ceolburh said tearfully.

"Fetch my cloak, Ceolburh," Ricole insisted.

"If you must go, my lady, at least allow me to fetch guards to accompany and protect you," Ceolburh pleaded as she wrapped the hooded cloak around her determined mistress.

"To protect me?" Ricole laughed scornfully. "Who, among my people, can I trust but you, Ceolburh? Freya, and none other, shall protect me."

*   *   *

The moon was full and bright, and lighted the quarter of a mile track that led through the forest to the Sacred Grove. Her hand on her knife-hilt, making a determined effort to ignore the sense of impending evil which beset her as she traversed the denser part of the forest where the moonlight penetrated the thick foliage only in patches, Ricole arrived at last at the Sacred Grove.

She at once saw the warriors who, chattering and laughing, were grouped around the post outside the temple. She hastened towards them and addressed Morcar.

"This is an outrage!" she cried angrily.

"My lady!" Morcar exclaimed in astonishment, as soon as he saw her. "What brings you here alone at such an hour. 'Twas hardly wise to. . . ."

"Unbind the lord Woden at once," Ricole interposed. "He is our people's guest and you dishonour them by flouting the laws of hospitality in this manner."

"The Witenagemot is to meet again upon the morrow to elect a new chieftain, my lady," Morcar told her. "At such a time, we can permit no stranger to wander freely among us. Who knows what treachery he may have planned!"

"Treachery?" Ricole asked, scornfully. "You are over-imaginative, Morcar. Why should you suspect the lord Woden of treachery?"

"Because, as I have said, he is a stranger, and a stranger is not welcome here at such a time."

"Has he shown signs of constituting a threat to our people?" Ricole demanded.

"He will have no opportunity of so doing, my lady, for I, Morcar, shall prevent it."

"What mean you, Morcar?" Ricole asked coldly, recognising the threat behind Morcar's words.

"The number nine has some curious significance for my lord Woden," Morcar answered with a malicious grin. "Did he not appear among us at the ninth hour? Did we not see the raven encircle the boat nine times before it permitted you to tend him?"

"And?" asked Ricole fearfully.

"The lord Woden shall hang for nine nights on the windswept tree yonder, my lady."

"The sacred tree?"

"The sacred tree, my lady," Morcar acknowledged. "He

shall be offered as a sacrifice to the gods."

"But now is not the time for sacrifice, as well you know, Morcar," Ricole said with asperity. "You mean to murder him."

"Murder him?" Smiling wickedly, Morcar shook his head. "Who spoke of murdering him? You are the one who is over-imaginative now, my lady. He will merely be hanged on the tree for nine nights—and days of course— and then he will be cut down."

"None can survive hanging for more than a few minutes," Ricole pointed out.

"You misunderstand me, my lady. Woman-like, you jump to the most alarming conclusions," Morcar said mockingly. "The lord Woden will not be hanged by the neck. His body will be bound to the tree with ropes, and iron nails will secure his hands and feet."

"Morcar, as my lord father's daughter, I beg you for the release of this man," Ricole pleaded earnestly.

"It cannot be, my lady," Morcar replied.

Ricole turned to Cerdic.

"Cousin Cerdic, I appeal to you as my kinsman to have mercy on this man who is the honoured guest of our people," she said.

"And if I so do, how will you reward me, cousin?" Cerdic enquired. "Will you promise before these witnesses to become my bride?"

Ricole heard Morcar's angry cry of protest at Cerdic's words and realised as never before how precariously balanced was the peace between her people.

She turned in desperation to another cousin, Osbern.

"What of you, my kinsman?" she asked. "Will you, son of my father's brother, speak in defence of the lord Woden, or have you also your own interests to serve?"

"Son of your father's brother, you say?" asked Osbern

dispassionately. "My father was indeed your father's brother, the elder brother Leofgar slew in order to make himself chieftain. You shall receive no assistance from me, cousin."

"Alas, Osbern, the happening of which you speak is long past," Ricole reminded him gently.

"Past, my cousin?" Osbern asked, his eyes hard and uncompromising. "The past is the progenitor of the present, just as my father was my progenitor. But for the evildoing of your father in slaying mine, I would now be chieftain, my sons would be my heirs, and none could gainsay us. I am rightfully the man to take Earl Leofgar's place. I have recently become a widower. If I assist you now, will you promise to become my bride and thus assist me to regain my rightful inheritance?"

"Enough of this play-acting," cried Morcar furiously, before Ricole could reply. "Think you I would stand by and permit our late lamented lord's only daughter to promise herself to her cousin? Would I see the laws of the gods flouted, and bring down their curse upon us all? Do our people want an atheling who is deaf and dumb, who has four legs and a furry tail?"

Why, thought Ricole distractedly, must they all choose this inauspicious moment to remind me of marriage and child-bearing? She glanced towards the fettered Woden and met his gaze. His gaze seemed locked with hers, as if in silent communication. His expression was inscrutable, impossible to read. He appeared to have accepted his situation, for he was neither attempting to free himself from the chains nor pleading for mercy, though he must have overheard Morcar telling her of his fate.

It was then, in those fleeting moments of anguish and indecision, that Ricole recognised the truth. Woden was the man she wished to marry. If she could not marry

Woden, love him, bear his children, then she would marry no one, love no one, bear no children. If she could not marry Woden, she would die sooner than marry another.

"I shall marry none of you!" she cried passionately. "I have already made that clear to Morcar and I declare it now in front of you all. I would kill myself rather than take any one of you for my husband!"

Morcar, who had seen her expression as she had gazed at Woden, was suddenly consumed by jealousy.

"The stranger must die," he said uncompromisingly.

"I beg you spare him, Morcar," Ricole pleaded.

"He shall have his freedom if you will relinquish yours— that is my price," Morcar said inexorably.

"Marry you, you mean?"

Morcar nodded but said nothing more, watching her cynically.

Could I marry Morcar, even to save Woden? Ricole thought to herself. A moment ago methought I would kill myself rather than marry any man but Woden. But if Woden dies because I would not sacrifice myself to save him, because I refuse to marry Morcar, then shall not I be guilty of Woden's death?

She turned despairingly to Woden.

"Lord of the raven, pray tell me what I must do. I do not, cannot, love this man, any of these men. I, Ricole, love another. But if I refuse them, they will kill you."

"They will kill me only if the sky gods permit it, my lady," Woden told her calmly. "The sky gods are all-powerful and far-seeing, and can easily overcome the puny schemes of evil men. Follow your heart, my lady. Follow your heart and save yourself for the man you love."

"You do not understand, lord of the raven," Ricole said tearfully. "How could you understand? Even I can scarcely believe it. The man I love is. . . ."

Woden coolly interrupted. "The sky gods see into the hearts of men. They see the evil that is in the hearts of these men, just as they see the love that is in yours. Go to the temple, my lady. Pray to Allfather, to Freya, and to the sky gods. They will console you in your distress and give you your heart's desire."

Weeping uncontrollably then, since she imagined that Woden did not see himself as the subject of her love, Ricole turned to Morcar.

"You are a cruel monster," she said bitterly. "To save the life of this man, I must consent to be your bride. You leave me no choice."

"We always have a choice, little one," insisted the voice of Woden, "if we also have the courage."

"What matters my freedom if it will save your life?" wept Ricole.

"What is life without freedom, little one?" Woden asked.

"But. . . ."

"I know what lies in your heart," Woden said gently. "I knew before you knew it yourself. Remember that and trust me."

"Then you do not wish me. . . ."

Woden interrupted firmly. "Leave it to me, little one, and I promise you that all will be well. When they have taken me to the tree, go to the temple and pray for the future of your people. Pray that the gods will send them a leader who will overrule the evil ones, and pray that you will find love and happiness, that you will give love and happiness."

Beside himself with rage at Woden's intervention, at his calm demeanour and the influence he clearly had upon Ricole, Morcar struck the shackled man twice across his face with the back of his hand. Blood poured from Woden's nose and a cut lip and, sobbing with anguish, Ricole turned and fled from the scene.

Ricole made towards the temple which, empty at this hour of the night, consisted of a large open chamber with a wooden floor, its focal point the larger-than-life statue of Freya which stood at the far end. Weeping with sorrow and distress, she flung herself at the feet of the statue.

She gazed up at the calm beautiful face of the goddess, at the tender compassionate gaze of the eyes, at the hand held out in blessing, and slowly she found tranquillity returning to her. She remained on her knees for a long time, how long she never knew, until her sobbing ceased and she felt the beauty and stillness of the temple taking hold of her, enveloping her in its peace.

She prayed then: for her unhappy people, that the gods would send them a worthy chieftain; for Woden, lord of the raven, that he might be given strength to bear his torment, that his enemies would not destroy his noble spirit, that his suffering, alone out there in the cold darkness, would soon be over; for herself, that, denied the man she now realised she loved above all else, the man who had been but a brief interlude in her life, the gods in their mercy would hasten her departure to the Other World.

She finished her prayers and then made her way to the door of the temple, unsure of her next move but driven by a curious impulsion to see for herself what had befallen Woden.

She went out into the cold air of the Sacred Grove, a grove that the moon had transformed into a greenwood of fairy-tale beauty, and made towards the giant tree. Evergreen and of a great age, its roots and branches spreading grotesquely in all directions, the tree situated on the fringe of the forest, dominated the Sacred Grove. It was a sacred tree, used for human sacrifice during the fertility festivals, and it symbolised the World Ash Tree, Yggdrasill, the legendary tree which was believed to support the Seven Worlds of the Universe. Midgard, the earth, was the middle one of these seven worlds and lay between Asgard, the heavenly home of the gods, and the Underworld ruled by the goddess Hel. The Earth was surrounded by seas wherein dwelt the Great Serpent which held its tail in its mouth, and on the outermost shores of the seas lay the mountain ranges of Giantland. The clouds had been created by the Frost Giants when they had flung the brains of Ymir, one of the giants, to the winds.

Morcar and the warriors had departed to the burgh for slumber, leaving only two trusted warriors to guard their victim, confident that they had satisfactorily disposed of Woden. He would be dead, they had told themselves, by morning.

When Ricole reached the tree, she saw that Morcar and his companions had done their work well. Woden's body was bound by a rope to the massive trunk of the great tree, his arms were spread out along two strong branches and were nailed palm outwards, whilst his feet likewise had been nailed to the trunk of the tree. His eyes were closed, he was silent, neither moan nor complaint issuing from his lips, and he appeared to have lost consciousness.

Ricole sat on the mossy ground at the foot of the tree for a long time. Oblivious of the cold and her aloneness, of her danger as a lone woman in the forest, of danger from man, wolf, or wild boar, she was conscious only of her misery and of Woden's dreadful suffering. The man who lay in helpless agony before her, was the man she loved, the only man she had ever loved, the only man she would ever love: despite her youth and inexperience Ricole was convinced of those things in a way that she had never been convinced of anything else in her life.

She had been sitting there for a considerable time before

she became aware of a whirring noise high up above in the tree. She had heard the sound before but had paid it no attention, imagining it to be a bat, or some other nocturnal creature, going about its business. But then she caught sight of Huginn silhouetted against the moonlit sky. As she watched, the raven flew nine times around the tree and then perched motionless and silent upon one of the branches. Ricole was reminded of the boat and how Huginn had guarded Woden then as he had lain unconscious. Had not Woden told her that Huginn guarded him only whilst he was asleep or unconscious? Did that explain why Huginn had made no attempt to defend Woden when he had been taken captive by Morcar and the warriors? It was all very puzzling.

Her cloak wrapped closely round her to keep out the cold night air, Ricole must have fallen asleep, for she awoke later to find that a new day had dawned. She stood up, smoothed her crumpled petticoats, and moving closer, gazed upward at the figure hanging against the tree.

Woden's eyes were closed and sunken, his face showed a deathly pallor, and the blood which had dripped from the wounds in his hands and feet and had formed small scarlet pools upon the ground beneath, had ceased to flow. Is he dead? Ricole asked herself. The guards, who had also snatched a few hours sleep, came forward then to inspect their prisoner. At once, there was an ominous rushing and whirring sound in the tree, as Huginn spread his wings wide and swooped down at the men, narrowly missing the eyes of one and scoring a deep gash across his brow. Huginn circled the tree and then swooped again, his powerful wings widespread as before. This time the other man flung his hands in instinctive protection across his face, and received a deep and bloody gash on his forearm instead. Huginn next circled the tree and its victim nine times more before perching in silent immobility upon a branch above Woden's head.

It was plain to both Ricole and the injured guards that Huginn at least was very much alive. Was he guarding his master in death?

Grief-stricken and despairing, Ricole at last made her way back to the burgh where she shut herself in her bower, refusing to see anyone. She wept inconsolably for a long time, weeping for what might have been and beset by doubts about the rightness of her own actions.

Am I culpable for Woden's death? she asked herself. Could I alone have saved the man I loved? I should not have hearkened to his brave words. He sought to help me, to make my decision easier for me. I ought to have disregarded his advice and made a pact with Morcar: I ought to have agreed to become Morcar's bride if he released Woden. That way I could have saved Woden from that cruel death. Now Woden is dead, and I wish I were dead also. My people are in no better case than before. What has Woden's sacrifice availed them? What has it availed him? What has it availed me? In time I shall be forced to marry Morcar or one of my cousins. I have merely postponed the evil hour.

SEVEN

Ricole remained in her bower for the next eight days, partaking of only sufficient food to keep herself alive, refusing to see anyone but Ceolburh, and weeping for hours at a time in inconsolable grief at her double bereavement. She knew nothing of what was going on in the rest of the burgh. She did not know if a new chieftain had been elected, or if Morcar was virtually ruler of the tribe. Of Morcar himself she had seen nothing since she had sent him a message by Ceolburh, begging that he would respect her grief. She had requested that she be left alone to mourn in private for the death of her father, and to recover from the shock of the murder of her guest, until the nine days of Woden's hanging had passed.

In the evening of the eighth day, Ceolburh informed her mistress that Morcar had requested admittance to her bower.

"Requested?" asked Ricole in surprise. "Has Morcar then had a change of heart? Methought it was his custom to take what he wanted."

"There's much unrest in the tribe, my lady," Ceolburh explained. "The Witenagemot has not yet chosen a new leader, for the Witan are deeply divided. Your kinsmen, my lady, have banded together against Morcar and control some of the warriors, but Morcar ignores their authority and still controls the *hearth-horde*."

"An unhappy situation indeed!" commented Ricole

wearily.

"Hoping to wean the remaining warriors to his side, Morcar is treading warily at present," Ceolburh went on. "Olaf tells me that Morcar fears an open confrontation with your kinsmen, until he has increased his following."

"There is no honour amongst murderers. Morcar and my kinsmen were united enough in murdering the lord Woden," Ricole said bitterly. "I will see Morcar now—there is no point in postponing the evil moment. Show him in, Ceolburh."

Leaving a strong guard outside the door, for he knew he went in danger of his life, Morcar, wearing a leather patch over his right eye socket, entered Ricole's bower and bowed courteously.

"I trust I find you in good health, my lady," he said.

"For a maiden who would rather be dead, I am, alas, in alarmingly good health," Ricole answered discouragingly.

"The stranger will be taken down from the tree at the sixth hour tomorrow morning, my lady," Morcar told her.

"Why tell me that, Morcar?" Ricole asked. "Have you come here merely to taunt me? You murdered the lord Woden. You murdered an honoured guest without cause or provocation."

"Your expression as you gazed upon his face was provocation enough for any man who desires you as I do, my lady."

"My expression?" asked Ricole coldly. "You were provoked by my compassion for a doomed man?"

"It was passion rather than compassion I read in your expression then, my lady," Morcar said incisively.

Ricole flushed. "I once had respect for you, as had my lord father. I recognised your ability as a warrior, even though . . ."

"Even though you did not desire me as a lover?" interposed Morcar. "Have no fear on that account, my lady! Once you are my bride, I shall soon overcome your scruples."

"Can even you overcome the scruples of a dead woman, Morcar?" Ricole asked, derisively. "Nay, I no longer even respect you."

"You hate me perchance?" Morcar asked, interestedly. "When a woman lies with a man, hate and love are close kin to each other. Did not you know that? Alas, how could you know—you are yet a virgin! A spirited maiden, like a spirited filly, is always a provocation—'twill be my pleasure to tame you."

"I do not even hate you, Morcar," Ricole managed to say with a calm she was far from feeling. "I have nothing but contempt for you."

Morcar shrugged. "Disappointing as the knowledge may be for you, my lady, I did not come here to discuss our love-hate relationship. I came here to tell you about the removal of the stranger's corpse, lest you should wish to be there."

"There? In the Sacred Grove?" Ricole asked, in a shocked tone. "To see the results of your handiwork?"

"There is talk of many people gathering in the Sacred Grove on the morrow, my lady," Morcar told her. "Our people, it seems, cannot resist a spectacle and. . . ."

"A spectacle?" asked Ricole in horror. "They wish to gloat over the remains of a cruelly murdered guest?"

"Our people grow increasingly uneasy in the present climate of uncertainty. I hope shortly to bring about a coup, to seize the chieftainship and bring stability to the tribe."

"The gods will surely not permit it!" Ricole declared, hopefully.

"There are whispers of curious happenings in the Sacred

c

Grove since the stranger was hanged. Mere superstition of course, my lady," Morcar said lightly, "but doubtless our people are eager to see for themselves that all is well."

"Of what curious happenings do you speak?" asked Ricole.

" 'Tis rumoured that voices have been heard in the clearing when no one appears to be there, and that curious droning sounds have been heard. And always there is the raven," Morcar explained. "Some say that the stranger is not dead. Blood of Tiw! Not dead? After nine nights in the chill forest, bleeding from wounds and without food and water!"

"Must you remind me?" protested Ricole, shuddering.

"Methought you also might doubt the death of the stranger, my lady."

"Would that I could, Morcar!" exclaimed Ricole. "Doubtless our people fear the vengeance of the gods for our guest's murder, and seize on the impossible hope that he is yet alive."

"Then you have no doubt of his death?" Morcar asked, tauntingly. "You do not wish to discover the truth for yourself?"

Ricole gazed shrewdly at him. Do I detect a note of unease in Morcar's voice? she thought to herself. Has he been affected by the rumours and whisperings of others? Has he a conscience after all? 'Tis almost as if he is seeking reassurance from me, as if my refusal to believe the rumours would relieve his own anxiety.

"I shall be there in the Sacred Grove at the sixth hour, Morcar," she said then, and was rewarded by his dismayed expression. "I will be there to curse you for your handiwork!"

After Morcar had left the bower, Ricole flung herself down on her couch, her body shaking with sobs. Why will

Morcar not leave me in peace? she thought to herself. He
came here merely to taunt me, to gloat upon my unhappi-
ness. Is he not content with having destroyed the man I
loved? It is plain that he recognised my feelings for Woden,
and was jealous—that must surely be the answer.

As she lay there and the minutes passed into hours, and
the hours passed into a new day, bringing her nearer to the
moment she dreaded when she must carry out her determination to join her people in the Sacred Grove, Ricole
seemed to gather a new strength. Perchance the gods
have not deserted me, she thought. Perchance they will
bring good out of evil, will bring security for my people
out of my grief. Perchance when my people see Woden's
dead body and recognise Morcar for the villain he is,
they will unite against him and force the Witenagemot
to elect a new chieftain from one of the older, wiser men
of the tribe. To this end and in defiance of Morcar who
plainly thought me given over entirely to grief, I shall put
on a bold front. I shall go to the Sacred Grove, my grief
carefully hidden. I shall be dressed in finery such as befits
Earl Leofgar's daughter, the better to use my influence for
the benefit of my people.

As the sixth hour approached, with Ceolburh's willing
assistance, Ricole put on a white undergown, a pale blue
overgown with an embroidered hem and front panel, a dark
red mantle fastened with gold cords, and a white head-rail
which covered her blonde hair and was held in place with
a gold fillet. She then summoned her handmaidens and,
keeping a tight rein on her emotions, walked at a leisurely
pace to the Sacred Grove.

The crowd made way for Ricole as soon as she was
recognised and she walked forward until she was standing
at the foot of the windswept tree, the tree which bore the
corpse of the man she had known and loved for so short a

space of time. She gazed up at the pale, motionless figure whose eyes were closed and sunken. The air in the Sacred Grove seemed still and oppressive. Even the wind seems to have deserted the giant tree, she thought, and there is no sign of Huginn.

The appointed hour having arrived, accompanied by the *hearth-horde*, Morcar appeared on the scene and at once addressed the multitude.

"People of Angel," he said sonorously, "you see before you a dead man."

There were murmurs from among the crowd at this, although whether of approbation or disapproval it would have been difficult to say.

"There are those among you, I am told, who fear witch-craft, who suspect that the stranger is not yet dead," Morcar continued. "Look at him, my friends: does not he look dead? He looks dead, dead as mutton, to me, but to satisfy those among you who have doubts, I shall conduct an experiment. This spear I am holding, a weapon of unusual size and skilful workmanship, was discovered by me in the ship which bore the stranger hither. . . ."

Ricole gasped in dismay and was quite unable to remain silent in the face of such an outrage.

"You went to the ship, Morcar?" she asked breathlessly.

"I went to the ship, my lady."

"Despite my assurance to the lord Woden that its contents would remain undisturbed, you went to the ship and took the spear?" Ricole asked, angrily.

"The stranger is dead, and dead men need no weapons," Morcar answered evenly.

"Did you take aught else?" Ricole enquired.

"Nay, but I shall return to the ship after our little ceremony here is over," Morcar said glibly. "The ship intrigues me for I confess I have never seen its like before."

"Now that you have appropriated the dead man's property, pray tell us what is your intention, Morcar?" Ricole asked, coldly.

"People of Angel, I shall climb up into the tree and shall pierce the stranger's side with this spear," Morcar announced. "That should convince you beyond all doubt that the stranger is dead."

White to the lips at such desecration of the dead, but restrained from voicing further protest by she knew not what, Ricole said no more. She watched in horror as, carrying the shining spear, Morcar climbed upon the back of one of the warriors and swung himself up into one of the tree's cross branches, the branch to which Woden's left hand was nailed. Crawling carefully along the sturdy branch, Morcar proceeded until he reached the lifeless body.

There was a moment or two of utter silence, of breathtaking suspense, as Morcar held on to the branch with his left hand for support, and drew back his right hand which held the spear. He poised the spear and then, with unerring aim, thrust it forward into his victim's left side.

A mixture of blood and water oozed slowly from the pierced side, signifying that the stranger was dead.

The stranger did not move.

The raven did.

As Morcar looked upward in sudden alarm, he saw Huginn, wings widespread, swooping down towards him. It was the last thing that Morcar ever saw. He screamed with pain as the raven's beak pierced his left eye, his remaining eye, and instinctively raised his left hand to ward off the attack. Still grasping the spear in his right hand, he plumped to the ground to lie like a sacrifice at the feet of his victim.

Morcar's warriors hastened to his aid. But Morcar was beyond their help. Morcar was dead. Oswy stooped to remove the blood-tipped spear from Morcar's grasp. At first it defied his attempts to retrieve it and he had forcibly to uncurl the fingers which held it. He removed the spear and then, with an obscene oath, dropped it hastily on the ground.

"Freya protect us!" he gasped. "Look at that, mates! Looks as if the spear's been heated over a mighty fire. It's still hot and on being pulled from Morcar's hand, it's taken some of his flesh with it!"

Their superstitious fears already increased by Morcar's sudden death and Oswy's astonishing words, the spectators fell to their knees, wailing and calling on the gods for protection at what happened next. Darkness began swiftly to descend upon the earth, just as it had done nine days previously, at the time of the stranger's arrival.

Ricole remained where she was, her eyes never leaving the dead face of Woden. Despite the panic and terror around her, she felt curiously at peace, and in the fast-fading light she registered the fact that Huginn was now perched at the top of the tree, high above the head of his master.

In a matter of seconds, bright sunlight had given way to darkness. The morning sky became black as on a moonless night, and a myriad of stars shone from the heavens.

Ricole could see nothing now. She could hear the voices and lamentations of her people, as they prayed to the gods for protection. No one moved, for no man could see his neighbour, and in that Sacred Grove in the heart of the forest, at the mercy of the wild creatures who dwelt therein, all knew instinctively that safety lay in numbers.

For three long hours, the darkness remained. Despite the anxiety around her, despite the knowledge that Morcar's dead body was lying only a few feet away from her and had narrowly missed her in its rapid descent from the tree,

Ricole felt calm and unafraid. The darkness offered her a cloak for her sorrow, and her people had become strangely unreal. The only reality, so it seemed to Ricole, was the lifeless figure which was still hanging on the tree.

From the sixth hour there was darkness over all of Angel until the ninth hour when, just as on that previous occasion, daylight suddenly returned and the sun shone as brightly as before.

At once, all eyes became riveted upon the still figure which hung from the tree. There were shouts and cries, expressions of anger and alarm which would not be silenced.

"The gods are angry—they have shown us their displeasure!"

"Our guest was dishonoured by Morcar—Morcar has paid the price!"

"For three hours the gods abandoned us to the powers of darkness! They sent Loki and his imps amongst us! Did you not feel their evil polluting the very air around us, friends? One of the churl's wives gave birth during the darkness—the woman is dead, but the child they say has neither arms nor legs!"

"What must we do to mitigate the wrath of the gods? Can no one tell us what we must do? We are a people accursed, people without a leader—who will come to our aid and protect us from the Evil One?"

Ricole turned to face her people. She spoke to them. She spoke with her own voice, but the words were not her words. They were the words of a stranger.

"People of Angel, do as I tell you and all will be well. The sky gods are angry but they will be appeased if you follow my instructions with care and reverence. Turn to the east, each one of you, and bow humbly nine times. *Ja*, that is good. Now repeat the following words after me:

'Eastwards we stand, for favours we pray
We pray the great Lord, we pray the mighty Prince
We pray the Holy Warden of the heavenly kingdom
To earth we pray and to sky-heaven.' "

The Angles obediently repeated the words after Ricole
and then waited for her to speak further. Was not the lady
Ricole the daughter of their beloved Earl Leofgar? Was not
she the child of his loins, flesh of his flesh? Was Leofgar
speaking to them through the lips of his daughter?

"Now, people of Angel," continued the voice of Ricole,
"turn three times sunwise and stretch yourself along the
ground full length and say the litany to Freya with me:

'Holy Freya, mother of the gods, pray for us,
Queen of heaven, pray for us . . .' "

As they recited the litany in unison, the crowd became
calmer, and looked to Ricole as their new leader. Is not she
a virgin and, as such, beloved of the gods? they asked themselves. Is not she pure and unspotted, renowned for her
gentleness and good works, for her care of the sick and the
old and the orphans?

The litany came to an end and this time Ricole remained
silent. She knew, with an intuitive wisdom she could not
have explained, that the next move must come from her
people themselves.

"Take the stranger down!" suddenly commanded Siferth,
Leofgar's brother.

"*Ja*, take him down and give him proper burial," agreed
many voices from the crowd.

At Siferth's signal, the warriors of the *hearth-horde* at
once stepped forward. Assisted by their comrades and keeping a wary eye on Huginn who seemed to be showing no
interest in this new development, two of the warriors

climbed on to the branches of the tree and carefully removed the nails from the hands and feet of the victim.
Whilst three of their number supported the body, the others
unbound the ropes which held it to the tree. The inert
form was lifted down and, in accordance with Ricole's
instructions, wrapped in a linen winding-sheet brought in
haste from the temple, and laid temporarily, the spear
beside it, in a nearby cave. A great boulder was placed
at the cave's entrance to protect the corpse from the
scavenging wolves until the morrow when, in accordance with custom, the dead man would be cremated on a
pyre.

EIGHT

The bewildering and dramatic events of the morning over,
Ricole and her people returned to the burgh where once
more she sought the peaceful solitude of her bower. So
much had happened in the past three hours, much that was
disturbing and inexplicable, although the removal of
Woden's hanging body had made her grief seem a little
more bearable.

Morcar was dead. No longer need she fear him and his
determination to possess her. All the same, was there
another man strong enough to rule her people? Their need
of a leader had never shown itself so forcibly as when,
after the sun's eclipse for the second time within nine days,
her people had hearkened to her voice as if to the exhorta-
tions of a goddess. Siferth and her other kinsmen had given
her their support, but still no man had come forward who
seemed fitted to take Leofgar's place.

Little as I knew of him, I believe in my innermost being
that Woden was such a man, Ricole said to herself. Had I
become his bride, I believe my people would have accepted
him as their chieftain and he would have ruled them with
strength and wisdom.

I knew him for so brief a time, alas. He came to Angel
as a stranger and he died a few hours later, no longer a
stranger to me, but the man I loved as I will never love
anyone else in my whole life. How small a space of time
we spent together, when I would gladly have remained with

him for the rest of my life. . . .

Exhausted by lack of sleep, by grief and anxiety, Ricole lay back upon her couch and drifted into a deep slumber.

But her slumber was not peaceful. It was beset by a disturbing dream, by sights and images which had some basis in reality but which seemed to become exaggerated into the fantasies of a nightmare.

She saw a dark sky. A ball of fire. A ship propelled by neither oars nor sails. She saw a spear of immense size which seemed to reflect the sunlight, which drew heat from the sun's rays and became red-hot. She saw a sword of such exquisite craftsmanship that it could well have been fashioned by the gods themselves: she had not seen its like before. Even my father did not possess a weapon of such beauty, she thought to herself.

She seemed to be floating on air and she could see the spear and the sword and the inside of a cave. 'Tis the cave on the edge of the forest where the body of Woden lies, she thought. But there is no body in the cave, and the stone has been rolled away from the entrance. She heard the howling of the wolves. Holy Freya! Who has removed the stone? she asked herself in horror. Did one of my kins-men, Cerdic or Osbern perchance, observe my regard for Woden as did Morcar? Have they been to the cave, re-moved the stone and left the body at the mercy of the wolves? Have the wolves already taken. . . .

"Woden!" she cried and awoke in terror.

Tears were streaming down her cheeks, her heart was beating suffocatingly in her breast, and her mind was beset by horror and distress.

What does it mean? she asked herself. Has something happened to Woden's body? Was it merely a dream—or a warning or premonition? I have slept for many hours, it seems, for it is nearing dusk. Holy Freya, tell me what I must do, she prayed fervently.

It was then that the curious idea came to her. Will the gods punish me for so doing? she wondered. But I must find out for myself if all is well. What a comfort it would be to look once more upon the face of my beloved, to wash the blood from his face, his hands, his feet, to implant a loving kiss upon his cold brow.

I shall tell no one where I am going. I have given orders that I am not to be disturbed till morning, and all I think will respect my wishes after the curious happenings of this morning. Even Ceolburh has been told not to disturb me, so no one will discover my absence, and I shall only be gone for a little while.

Ricole dressed herself in a plain white woollen gown, fastened her sheathed knife to her girdle for protection, and wrapped herself in a hooded fur-lined cloak to combat the cold evening air. She crept from her bower, left the chieftain's dwelling unseen, and made her way through a gap in the palisade towards the forest and the Sacred Grove.

She was half-way along the quarter of a mile track when the disconcerting thought struck her. What of the stone? she asked herself in dismay. How foolish of me! Influenced by the absence of the stone in my dream, I have been assuming it will no longer be there. It took four strong men to place it in position, and it would be impossible for me to move it on my own. Alas, I shall not after all be able to gaze upon the face of my beloved. I am journeying to the Sacred Grove in vain.

Tears filled her eyes but she brushed them impatiently aside. Nay, my journey will not be in vain. I shall kneel before the entrance to the cave and pray that the gods will smile lovingly upon the lord Woden as he journeys to the Other World. The gods, who have taken so much from me of late, will surely grant me this one request.

But when Ricole at last reached the cave, she found that the stone had indeed been rolled aside, just as in her dream. The mouth of the cave was open and unprotected.

Mother of the gods! she said to herself. What Loki's work is this? Have Cerdic or Osbern been here before me? Observing my regard for the lord Woden, did one of them in truth return with his followers and remove the stone, so that the body of my beloved should lie at the mercy of the wolves? Is there no end to the cruelty of men?

Dreading what she would see, haunted still by the dream which in retrospect bore all the hallmarks of a nightmare, Ricole stepped hesitantly into the dark interior of the cave.

The first thing she saw was Huginn. The second thing was that the interior of the cave was not dark as she had imagined. It was lighted by an oil lamp which shone on the empty wooden bier. As Ricole's horrified gaze fell on the unoccupied bier, she saw to her astonishment that it was draped with a large and luxurious animal skin, the skin of a white bear, rare and of great worth, and found only in the frozen wastes of the North.

It was then that she saw Woden.

Clad in an animal skin with a thick leather belt encircling his waist, Woden was gazing enigmatically at her. Fearing she was seeing an apparition, that the gods were punishing her for disturbing the resting-place of the dead, Ricole gasped and the blood drained from her face.

"Do not be afraid, little one," Woden said then. "There is nothing to fear. I have been waiting for you."

"You were waiting for me?" Ricole asked breathlessly, seating herself on the edge of the bier to still her trembling limbs. "But how could that be? How did you know I would come here?"

"I knew."

"Then I too must be dead," Ricole said tremulously.

"You are not dead, little one," smiled Woden. "Your cheeks have regained their colour now and they would not glow like that if you were dead, nor would your eyes shine with such lustre."

"In my dream I saw. . . ."

"I know what you saw in your dream, little one—it was that which brought you here," Woden interposed.

"Then—you—are—not—dead?" Ricole asked haltingly, as if she feared to hear the answer.

"I am not dead."

Ricole's joyful smile would surely have melted the coldest heart.

"Oh, my lord, how glad I am! I feared I had lost you, and I . . ." She hesitated, shy of expressing her feelings to a man who was almost a stranger.

"You feared you had lost the man you loved?" Woden asked, gently.

"You know that also?" Ricole asked, softly.

Woden nodded. "I know that also. You love me and I love you, little one. It had to be thus, for it was ordained thus."

"You are telling me that all that has happened is part of a plan. Whose plan?" Ricole asked, with a tiny puzzled frown. "I do not understand."

"Alas, little one, you ask so many questions, when all I want is to take you in my arms and love you. . . ."

Ricole interrupted hastily, her cheeks flushing. "My lord Woden, I beg you remember you are all but a stranger to me," she said demurely.

"In that which Man calls Time we are strangers, but do you not know in your innermost being that we belong to each other, that we have belonged to each other since the beginning of Time and shall so belong till the end of Time?"

"But. . . ."

"At this moment I desire you above all else, little one. I want to hold you close in my arms, so very close, and. . . ."

"My lord Woden," interrupted Ricole reprovingly. "Are you no better than Morcar and my cousin Cerdic?"

Woden smiled wickedly. "I am much better than Morcar and Cerdic, as I shall shortly prove to you."

"My lord, your hands!" Ricole cried, in astonishment.

"My hands?" he asked, not understanding.

"Where are the marks of the nails which pierced your hands and feet?"

"They have healed," Woden explained carelessly. "We have learned the art of rapid healing in the land whence I come."

"Whence did you come my lord?" asked Ricole curiously.

"If you ask any more questions, little one, I shall think you are rejecting my advances and that would never do!"

At that moment Ricole gave a cry of astonishment and pointed to the ground beside the bier.

"The sword!" she exclaimed in wonder. "The sword is here, just as it was in my dream. How came it here, my lord?"

"After I had retrieved Gungnir from the Sacred Grove. . . ."

"Gungnir?" interposed Ricole. "Who is Gungnir?"

"My spear is called Gungnir," Woden told her. "After I had retrieved it from the Sacred Grove, I betook myself to the boat-house on the shore and collected the sword."

Ricole gazed in fascination at the beautiful sword. Set in a scabbard of gold and garnet bosses, its gold pommel was set with garnets and crested by a gold boar. Its hilt was embossed with a design of skilfully-carved snakes that swirled against a background of niello, and its iron blade was inlaid with silver.

"It is very beautiful, my lord," she said admiringly. " 'Tis a masterpiece of craftsmanship—my lord father would have envied you such a sword."

"It is a very special sword, my lady. My people call it the Sword of Woden, for it is the defender of myself and my line and is useless in the hands of our enemies."

"What is the significance of the gold boar, my lord?" Ricole asked. "I should have thought a raven would have been a more fitting emblem."

"I cannot answer that question at the moment, little one," Woden said obscurely. "But you shall learn the answer in time."

"Your sword has magical properties, as has your spear, my lord?" Ricole asked, curiously.

"One could say that," Woden answered enigmatically.

"Both your sword and your spear have magical properties," Ricole said. "Have you no other weapons, my lord?"

"I have another weapon and if the gods will it, that other weapon will gain me my heart's desire, and achieve much," Woden said meaningfully.

"You mean. . . ." Ricole paused and eyed him shyly.

"*Ja*, that is what I mean, little one. Tonight here in this Sacred Grove, wherein I have dwelt these past nine nights, nights in which I have achieved magical secrets and powers, you will become mine."

"But we are not yet man and wife, my lord," Ricole reminded him. "We must wait until the morrow when we can go to the priest and be married in the temple."

Woden nodded. "On the morrow we shall go to the temple as you say. On the morrow, as soon as I have informed your people that I am their new chieftain, we will go to the temple and be married in the sight of all. But now we shall be married in our own eyes; we shall be united in body and in soul. You will become mine and will remain mine for eternity."

"For ever?" Ricole asked, breathlessly.

Woden nodded gravely. "For ever," he said.

"But how could that be? I do not understand."

"Just trust me, little one," Woden said quietly. "Trust me and let me love you. You will never regret so doing— you know that, do you not?"

Her gaze held by his, almost hypnotically Ricole pushed back her hood, untied the cords that held the edges of her cloak, and the laces and brooches that fastened the bodice of her gown. Woden gently drew her gown from her shoulders, exposing her breasts. He looked down at her, watching her expression as he touched her breasts.

"My lord . . ." she whispered, a little uncertainly.

"Is it not strange, little one, that you whose beauty surpasses that of every other woman I have seen, have never before known the carnal touch of a man, have never before known the delight of such caress?"

"Many men have desired me, my lord," Ricole murmured.

"Yet you waited for me. I know that. And now I am here and you are here and we need wait no longer. In nine months' time you will bring forth our first-born."

"Nine?" asked Ricole a trifle uneasily, as if reminded of something she would rather forget. "Morcar said that the figure nine had some special significance for you."

"At this moment it has but one significance," Woden said passionately.

Ricole felt her legs growing weak and her will dissolving into nothingness under his caressing hands.

Seeing this, Woden took the luxurious fur coverlet from the bier and placed it upon the winding-sheet which was already spread out on the floor of the cave. He drew her down on to it and soothed her with loving endearments and tender, knowing hands, which banished the last remnants of fear and the distress of the past nine days. She trusted Woden implicitly. She loved him with every fibre of her being. She was happy and secure in the arms of her lord. What more could she ask of the gods?

Ricole gasped once as he took her, and tears started involuntarily to her eyes.

"Pain and pleasure!" Woden murmured obscurely, as they became one.

NINE

Ricole awoke at the first light of dawn and for a few moments, so deep and peaceful had been her sleep, she was unable to recall where she was. She gazed around the cave in bewilderment but then, as memory returned and she recalled the events of the night, she smiled serenely and drew the warm fur coverlet more closely about her naked body. She could not remember falling asleep. She remembered the love-making, her joy and happiness in being held in the arms of the man she loved, and her own passionate response which had surprised her in its intensity. She stared up at the rocky roof, remaining still and silent for fear of disturbing the man who lay asleep beside her.

After a while, she turned very gently to look at Woden.

His eyes were wide open.

"My lord?" Ricole whispered. "You too are awake?"

"I am awake, little one," Woden answered. "I trust you are refreshed."

Ricole nodded. "*Ja*, my lord, but I cannot recall falling asleep."

"You fell asleep in my arms, exhausted at last by our love-making," Woden told her with a smile, placing a muscular arm around her and drawing her closer.

Ricole smiled and snuggled contentedly against him. " 'Tis such a joy being here with you, my lord," she said, but then she sighed.

"And yet you sigh, little one?" Woden asked, kissing

her cheek. "You are fearful of the coming day perchance?"

Ricole nodded. "So much lies in the balance, my lord. Many questions intrude upon my joy. Will my absence have been discovered? I ask myself."

"The lady Ricole, they tell me, is renowned for her piety—if she is observed returning from the Sacred Grove so early in the day, will not it be assumed that, distracted by the loss of her father and the inhospitable treatment of a guest, the lady Ricole has been seeking consolation in the temple?"

"*Ja*, my lord, you are right," Ricole smiled. "But that is not my chief concern. What of you, my lord? My people believe you are dead. They saw with their own eyes that you were dead. Will they accept you as their chieftain on your return, or will they fear you?"

"Should not a chieftain always be a little feared?" asked Woden thoughtfully.

"And what of my cousins, Cerdic and Osbern?" Ricole asked. "Morcar is dead, thanks be to Freya, but Cerdic and Osbern will show enmity towards any man who challenges their right to the chieftainship."

"They have a just claim?" Woden enquired.

"Osbern is the eldest son of the brother my father slew before he became chieftain," Ricole explained. "The gods never ceased to punish my father for his sin by denying him an heir, thereby bringing about our present unsettled state. Osbern has a strong claim—I cannot deny that."

"Osbern is a man of honour and wisdom?" Woden asked, quietly. "He is fitted to become chieftain?"

"Nay, that is what troubles me, my lord. Should either he or Cerdic become chieftain, each will constantly oppose the other. There would be continual strife and bloodshed, for we should be a divided people and thus would be at the mercy of the neighbouring tribes, the Saxons and the Jutes.

The Angles would not long survive as a people."

"Osbern and Cerdic are men of courage, and skilful warriors?" asked Woden.

"Both are renowned for their courage and battle skills, my lord."

"Then they will be useful men to serve a new chieftain," Woden said complacently.

"They will never so do," Ricole insisted. "Do not be deceived, my lord. They will oppose you utterly if you become chieftain and you will be in continual danger. Alas, my lord, I should fear greatly for you."

"Return to the burgh now, little one, and remain in your bower till I send for you," Woden said firmly. "Fear not, for I promise that all will be well. Call your maid when you reach your bower, tell her you are to marry the new chieftain today, and then be attired in your bridal array."

"What if you are not accepted as chieftain, my lord?" Ricole asked.

"Just trust me and do as I say, my lady," Woden said resolutely, getting to his feet and helping Ricole to hers.

Conscious now of her nakedness as she stepped from under the fur coverlet, Ricole blushed under her lover's amused and interested gaze, and hastily drew on her discarded gown and fur-lined cloak.

"Before you go, my lady, I shall present you with your *morgengyfu*,"[1] Woden said then.

"But surely my lord. . . ."

"Did you think I had no *morgengyfu* for you?" Woden interrupted, with a smile. "Stand still and close your eyes. . . . Now, my lady, I pray you open them again and behold your *morgengyfu*."

Ricole stared at the sword that Woden was offering her,

[1] Morning-gift: a present customarily given to a bride by her husband on the morning after the marriage was consummated.

hilt foremost, in astonishment.

"But that is your sword—it is your most beautiful possession, my lord," she protested.

"You are my most beautiful possession, little one," Woden insisted. "Take it—it is yours."

"But it is your most precious weapon," Ricole demurred.

"I have a more precious weapon, my lady, and that is yours also," Woden told her with a smile.

Ricole flushed, understanding his meaning. "But why are you giving me your sword?"

"It is a sword of rare worth and is therefore a suitable gift for the woman I love," Woden explained. "I myself carry only my spear."

"I fail to understand, my lord," Ricole said in perplexity. "All warriors have a sword, shield and battle-axe, as well as a spear."

"I am not 'all warriors', my lady," Woden smiled. "I am Woden, lord of the raven, who needs only his spear."

"Then why did you bring the sword to Angel?"

"I brought it for you, beloved."

"How could that be? You did not know of my existence," Ricole pointed out.

"Alas, more questions!" exclaimed Woden, sighing ostentatiously. "My lady asks so many questions, and seems forgetful of the fact that there is much to be done this day! All the same, lest my lady begins to doubt my regard for her, I will take precious time to explain about the sword. As you noticed last night, beloved, it bears the emblem of a boar. The boar, the black boar, will be the emblem of my first-born son and will hold a special significance for him. I am therefore presenting the sword to you, the mother of my first-born son. It will protect you, the mother of the lord of the black boar, from harm and when you no longer have need of it, you in turn will present it to our son."

Ricole's eyes were bright with emotion. " 'Tis a very beautiful gift: I shall treasure it always and hold it in trust for our son," she said softly.

She took the sword and carefully placed it in its scabbard which lay on the bier. Then she turned to Woden and, entwining her arms lovingly around his neck, she drew his mouth down to hers.

"I love you oh so dearly, my sweet lord," she murmured. "How can I ever thank you for all the joy and happiness you have brought me?"

"By loving me as much as I love you, little one. And...." Woden paused tantalisingly.

"And, my lord?" Ricole asked, a trifle anxiously.

"By refraining from asking so many questions," he said teasingly.

"But. . . ."

Woden's handsome face was suddenly serious. "So far you have taken me on trust, Ricole, daughter of Leofgar. Your love for me is as mine for you, and it overcame your scruples and your doubts. In the years ahead, there will be much you will not understand. Much must lie unexplained between us. The measure of your love for me, must be the measure of your trust in me. If I am to achieve my purpose here amongst the Anglian people, as achieve it I must, much will be unexplained until the sun sets on our last day at Angel."

"Our last day?" Ricole asked, tremulously. "The day of your death, or mine, do you mean? I beg you, my lord, do not speak of death when you have only just returned from death."

"One day when I have accomplished my mission here, I shall take you away from Angel, far away to the land of my people," Woden explained earnestly. "Then all will be made clear to you. Till then, beloved, you must love me and trust me. Can you do that?"

"Love you? How could I help loving you, my lord?" Ricole asked, passionately. "Life without you would be meaningless for me. And do not love and trust go hand in hand?"

"Then you agree?" Woden asked, quietly.

"To ask no more questions? I promise I shall ask no more questions, my lord—" Ricole smiled mischievously. "—or not too many anyway!"

"Little one, it is time you hastened back to the burgh," Woden said urgently. "Should your absence be discovered, your kinsmen would be greatly alarmed and a search would be made for you. That must not happen, for I do not wish to be discovered, alive and well, until the auspicious moment."

Ricole sighed. "Alas, my lord, how hard it is to say farewell, even for a little while! What if aught should go amiss and I should never see you again?" she asked tearfully.

"If the gods are on our side, who shall prevail against us?" Woden asked, kissing her fondly. "I have given you my son and my sword—they will suffice to give you courage till we are reunited."

"Farewell then, my lord, and may the gods protect you."

TEN

Later that same morning, the Witenagemot met in the council chamber which adjoined the Heorot. The Witan, which, led by Siferth, included all adult members of Earl Leofgar's family and numbered thirty members in all, sat on wooden seats around the circular chamber, further discussing the matter of the new chieftain. It was hoped, since Morcar was no longer there to oppose their wishes, that a new chieftain could be selected from amongst the older men of the tribe. Siferth himself, as Leofgar's closest surviving kinsman, was favoured by some members, but others were deterred by the knowledge that he was weak-willed and easily influenced by his sons.

One of the younger members rose to speak after Siferth's possible election had been discussed. "Cerdic, being strong-willed and having youth on his side would, in my opinion, be a better choice," he said.

At that, one of the elders rose to his feet. "Cerdic is quick-tempered and quarrelsome. His youth is against him, for he has not yet acquired wisdom and forbearance."

The subject of this discussion, himself a councillor, spoke angrily. "Are you suggesting that wisdom and forbearance are prerogatives of the old? Are we to replace Earl Leofgar with another chieftain with one foot in the grave? If so, we could well find ourselves again lacking a chieftain in a few weeks' time."

"It is greatly to be regretted that the gods denied Earl

Leofgar a son," put in Siferth, trying to pour oil on troubled waters.

"He has a daughter," Cerdic reminded him. "Whosoever becomes the husband of the lady Ricole, will also be the father of Earl Leofgar's grandsons—let us not forget that. Would not such a man be a suitable chieftain?"

"In speaking thus, you automatically eliminate yourself from the chieftainship, Cerdic," Siferth pointed out. "You already have a wife."

"I had a wife, my lord," Cerdic corrected him sadly. "She died this morning, alas!"

All turned to look suspiciously at Cerdic, for his reputation as a brutal husband with a growing dislike of his wife, was well known.

"Alas, Cerdic, this is grievous news! Permit me to offer you my heartfelt condolences," Siferth said steadily. "What sudden illness rendered you a widower?"

"My wife took her own life, the foolish woman!" Cerdic explained, sorrowfully. "She was of a jealous disposition, alas, as is well known and ofttimes accused me of fornication. When I returned to our dwelling in the early hours this morning, she became abusive, seized my sword from my belt and stabbed herself."

"Are you then in the habit of permitting any who will, to draw your sword, Cerdic?" enquired one councillor cynically. "Are you so slow to guard your own weapons, that you could not have prevented such a happening?"

Cerdic shrugged. "I was taken by surprise. One does not remain on personal guard in one's own dwelling. My wife is dead, alas, and talking will not bring her back to life! I mentioned the matter only in order to show that there is now no impediment to my marrying the lady Ricole."

At that instant, there were sounds of a disturbance beyond the entrance to the Witenagemot and the door was flung noisily open. The armed guards at the doorway had, it seemed, been tossed aside like corn in the wind, by the forbidding figure who strode into the chamber, armed only with a spear.

As the Witan turned as one man to survey the newcomer, hubbub broke out. There were cries and exclamations of astonishment, dismay, disbelief, superstitious fear, and of invocation to the gods for protection.

"Blood of Tiw! 'Tis the stranger!"

"The stranger is dead—did we not see his bleeding corpse with our own eyes? Holy Freya protect us, this must surely be an apparition!"

" 'Tis a judgement on us!"

"The gods show us their anger by sending the corpse here to confront us!"

"All the same, he does not look like a corpse!"

Striding to the centre of the chamber, Woden put up a peremptory hand and called for silence. There was an instant response to his command and he waited a full ten seconds before speaking further, seconds in which each man present was able to study to full effect the magnificent figure before him.

Woden's great height and muscular frame were perfectly proportioned. His shoulder-length blond hair and vivid green eyes contrasted strikingly with a complexion bronzed by exposure to sea and elements. He carried himself with an easy grace, a nobility, which set him apart from every other man there.

He was dressed in the ceremonial robes of a chieftain. He wore a knee-length tunic and a rectangular cloak, both of white material and exquisitely embroidered with gold at the edges of neckline and hem; and white hose which were cross-gartered from ankle to knee with gilded leather. He wore no ornaments other than the gold brooch on his right shoulder which fastened his cloak, and bore no weapons other than the shining spear in his left hand.

His blond masculine beauty, the white and gold of his raiment, and the shining spear, combined to produce an awe-inspiring effect, blending to such a brightness that light seemed to shine from him.

"Councillors of Angel," Woden said resonantly, "you see before you your new chieftain."

A further wave of sound spread through the Witenage-mot, as the Witan digested this astonishing information.

"You?" Cerdic, seemingly the first to recover his equilibrium, enquired. "*You* claim to be our new chieftain? Blood of Tiw!"

"I do so claim," Woden said coolly.

"But you are dead," Cerdic said grimly. "Did we not gaze upon your lifeless corpse? What Loki's trick is this that you now appear among us and claim the chieftainship?"

"I am not dead," Woden answered quietly.

"Not dead? After hanging for nine nights on a windswept tree?" Cerdic asked, incredulously.

"After nine nights, as you say, on a windswept tree, I am not dead," Woden said, smiling tolerantly. "What greater qualification could you look for in a chieftain?"

"We have been tricked," said Osbern, for once allying himself with Cerdic. "You were dead and now you are alive. Even if the Witan were to accept that as the truth, how would it give you the right to be chieftain? You are a stranger. You are not of the Angles."

"I was a stranger until ten days ago," Woden acknowledged. "Since then I have become well acquainted with the Angles. I have taken salt with you, I have died here among you, and I have returned to life among you. I am scarcely a stranger now."

"That may be so," Siferth said, addressing Woden for the first time. "But by what right do you claim to be chieftain? You are not of our people, lord of the raven. Whence come you?"

"The sky gods sent me," Woden answered calmly.

"The sky gods guided you here, you mean?" asked Siferth curiously. "When your ship was tossed by stormy seas and your companions were drowned?"

Woden seemed not to have heard the question.

"Besides it being the will of the sky gods, I have another claim to the chieftainship—one which transcends that of every other man in Angel," he said quietly.

"We would hear it, my lord," Siferth said courteously.

"Nine moons hence I shall become the father of Earl Leofgar's grandson," Woden said.

"Blood of Tiw! The stranger is mad!" exclaimed Cerdic laughingly. "He is not dead—we were mistaken in so thinking. His endurance is beyond that of most men but the suffering inflicted on him has clearly robbed him of his wits!"

Siferth was not amused. "I pray you explain your meaning, lord of the raven," he said.

"Last night, in the sight of the sky gods, the lady Ricole became mine," Woden answered.

"The stranger is indeed mad, as Cerdic says!" cried Osbern angrily. "There is not a man here who, knowing the lady Ricole to be a maiden of unblemished virtue, a virgin beyond reproach, could accept such a statement. The suggestion is preposterous."

"She became yours, you say, stranger?" snarled Cerdic. "If such is the case, then doubtless she was violated, taken against her will."

As the murmuring in the council chamber grew to an uproar at Cerdic's accusation, Woden strode to the doorway and called to one of the guards.

"Go at once to the lady Ricole's dwelling and tell her that her lord bids her come to the Witenagemot," he said.

As the guard departed on his errand, the Witan waited uneasily during the five minutes it took Ricole to answer the summons. All eyes seemed riveted on Woden, as if the councillors hoped to read the truth in his face, whilst he remained standing in the centre of the chamber, seemingly relaxed and untroubled by the doubts and hostility around him.

Ricole entered the Witenagemot to gasps of astonishment and admiration from the councillors.

She was dressed in bridal attire, in a white gown and head-rail, both lavishly embroidered with gold, and glittering with gold ornaments; in attire that matched the white and gold apparel of Woden.

But it was not Ricole's clothing which held the attention of every man in the Witenagemot. Her cheeks were glowing with happiness, her eyes shone like liquid pools, her blonde hair hung down her back in a living cascade, and she was smiling with joy. But the joyful smile was directed at one man only : it was abundantly clear that for the lady Ricole at that moment there was no one in the assembly but Woden.

As Ricole advanced towards Woden, it was noticed that she was carrying a sword, an unsheathed sword, in her right hand. Without speaking, she placed the sword on the table in the centre of the council chamber, where it glittered and sparkled in a shaft of sunlight that shone through one of the narrow unglazed windows, and then she curtseyed to Woden.

"Whence came the sword, my lady?" asked Siferth, gazing at it as if fascinated by its beauty.

"That I do not know, my lord uncle," Ricole answered.

"But whence it came is of no importance to anyone here, since it now belongs to me."

"It is yours?" asked Siferth in surprise.

"It is my *morgengyfu* from the lord Woden," Ricole explained simply.

"Your *morgengyfu*!" exclaimed Cerdic furiously. "So that which the stranger told us is true—he has taken your maidenhead."

"Is this true, Ricole, daughter of my brother?" asked Siferth severely.

"The lord Woden took that which was willingly given, my lord uncle," Ricole said shyly, her long eyelashes veiling her downcast eyes from the probing gaze of the councillors. "Last night the lord Woden and I were united in the sight of the gods, and today we shall be united in the temple in the sight of you all. Already I carry my lord's son, Earl Leofgar's grandson."

"You speak foolishly, my lady," said Osbern scathingly. "How can you be certain of such a fact?"

Ricole looked helplessly at Woden, uncertain how to express herself.

"The lady Ricole carries Earl Leofgar's grandson," Woden said firmly to the Witan.

"You can prove such a statement?" Cerdic asked, mockingly.

"Nine moons from now it will be proven," Woden answered impassively.

"Because you have, as you say, begotten a child on the lady Ricole, an act doubtless inspired by Loki and his minions, you expect us to accept you as our chieftain?" demanded Cerdic.

"You will accept me as your chieftain because I am the only man who can lead you at this present time, who can bring strength and unity to the Anglian people," Woden answered resolutely. "My power and wisdom are great and, aided by the sky gods, I was able to overcome the grave, as well as the scruples of the lady Ricole."

"What say you, Ricole, daughter of my brother?" asked Siferth. "You have accepted this man as your lover. Would you also accept him as your chieftain?"

"He is my lord," Ricole answered quietly. "I love him and I trust him. Last night I gave myself willingly into his care and I know I will never regret so doing. Councillors of Angel, I beg that you will do likewise. Take Woden as your lord, love him and trust him, give yourselves willingly into his care and you will never regret it."

Siferth looked consideringly around the Witenagemot, as if he sought to read the minds of his fellow councillors. Many looked thoughtful, as if impressed by Woden's unexpected return and by Ricole's appeal. It is plain, Siferth thought, that the lord of the raven possesses god-given powers and attributes, and such a man would make a fine chieftain.

"My lord Woden," Siferth said, speaking as leader of the Witan, "I ask that you and the lady Ricole adjourn to the outer chamber in order that my fellow councillors and I can discuss this new development. You will be informed of our decision in due course."

ELEVEN

Fifteen minutes later, Woden and Ricole were invited to return to the Witenagemot, an assembly from which Cerdic and Osbern were now conspicuously absent.

As soon as they reached the centre of the chamber, Siferth, as representative of the Witan, came forward and knelt in homage before Woden.

"Earl Woden, lord of the raven, we the tribal councillors of Angel offer you our allegiance," he said, his use of the title 'Earl' signifying the chieftainship.

"I thank you my lord," Woden answered simply. "The Witan will have no cause to regret its decision."

"I pray you take your sword, my lord, in order that each councillor in turn may swear fealty to you," Siferth said.

"My spear will suffice," Woden said, taking his spear in his right hand and holding it out, point upwards, in front of himself.

Each of the Witan then stepped forward in turn and, placing his right hand firmly upon the shaft of the spear, swore fealty to his new chieftain.

As the last man stepped forward, the entrance door of the Witenagemot was flung noisily open to admit Cerdic and Osbern, and their henchmen.

All eyes, except those of Woden himself, turned to look warily at the newcomers, who advanced challengingly towards the new chieftain.

D

"I, Osbern, eldest son of Olaf who was murdered by Earl Leofgar, contest the chieftainship," Osbern said incisively.

"The incident of which you speak, Osbern, was many years ago," Siferth said firmly. "Your father, my own eldest brother, was not a man of wisdom. Although Leofgar's murderous action against his kinsman was a crime greatly abhorred by the gods, Leofgar paid for his crime in being denied an heir, and atoned for it in ruling the Angles with justice and wisdom. Under Leofgar's leadership, our tribe grew and prospered. It was no longer a small tribe at the mercy of Saxon marauders from the south, who plundered our lands, and robbed us of our livelihood, our cattle, our women, and our lives. Do we wish for a return of the times that preceded Leofgar's rule? To those of us who are old enough to recall those days, such is unthinkable, a situation to be avoided at all costs. But let us not delude ourselves. That will be our fate unless we are ruled by one who can give us unity and stability. The Witan believes the lord Woden to be such a one."

"The lord Woden is a stranger," protested Osbern. "He is a man from the sea of whom we know nothing."

"We know that the gods, in preserving his life against tremendous odds, look with favour upon him," pointed out one of the councillors.

"The gods? Trickery, more like!" exclaimed Osbern scathingly. " 'Tis well known that Loki in the form of a raven, haunted the Sacred Grove during the nine nights of the stranger's ordeal—his apparent death and resurrection were clearly the work of the devil."

"The Witan has already discussed the matter in great detail," Siferth said resolutely, "and has concluded that the gods granted Earl Woden special powers."

"Special powers?" asked Cerdic scornfully. "Special powers indeed! The Witan sees signs of divine favour in a man who carries neither sword, shield, nor battle-axe—a primitive who has learned only to master a spear? Like Osbern, I too cannot accept the stranger as chieftain."

Woden, who had been listening to this exchange with an inscrutable expression, spoke for the first time.

"My lord Cerdic," he said evenly, "I suggest that the gods be given an opportunity of declaring themselves. You contest the chieftainship, you say? Then let us fight in open combat and let the gods decide the issue."

"A brawl?" asked Cerdic derisively. "With what do we fight—spears or our bare hands?"

"I shall fight with my bare hands," Woden answered coolly.

"Bare hands!" scoffed Cerdic. "No Anglian warrior fights with his bare hands. We are not churls, my lord."

"I am not an Angle, my lord, and therefore am not bound by rigid rules of warfare," Woden pointed out. "You may choose your weapons and I shall oppose you with my bare hands. A warrior needs no other weapon, if the gods are on his side."

"You expect the gods to defend you against sword, spear and battle-axe—and without even a shield to protect you?" chortled Cerdic.

"If by so doing, the gods can prove my superiority, my fitness to be chieftain, then I know I can count on their protection," Woden said quietly. "Do you swear to offer me your allegiance when I have overpowered you?"

Cerdic laughed mockingly. "*Ja*, my lord, when you have overpowered me thus, then will I offer you my allegiance," he said, confident of the outcome, and to cries of "Shame!" from the Witan.

Since it was the inviolable rule that one must prove one's point in words only in the Witenagemot, all the company adjourned to the square outside the Heorot.

Ricole, who had remained silent throughout Woden's exchange with Cerdic, was looking pale and nervous now, and she spoke anxiously to Woden as he was about to leave the council chamber.

"My lord," she said, "I fear greatly for you. Cerdic is renowned for his battle skills and, without a sword and spear for attack, and a shield to guard you, I fear he will tear you to pieces, alas. I beg you arm yourself for the fight."

"Retire to your dwelling, my lady," Woden said gently, ignoring her plea. "When the challenge has been met, I shall come to you."

Ricole's eyes filled with tears. "But what if. . . ."

Woden interrupted decisively. "I shall come to you in your dwelling. Whilst you await me, fill your mind with joyful thoughts. Think of us going to the temple where soon, hand in hand and watched by all our people, we shall become man and wife. Think of tonight when we shall be alone together and I shall hold you once more in my arms."

"How can I dwell upon such joys when I know I may lose you, my lord?" Ricole wept. "I could not bear it if, after all, you were taken from me."

"I shall come to you soon as I said," Woden insisted. "Did you not promise to trust me as well as love me? Go now, little one, and be at peace."

As Ricole obediently went her way, Woden left the Witenagemot to join Cerdic in the square where, word having got around, a crowd of warriors and churls had already mustered.

Cerdic and Osbern and their followers laughed mockingly when they saw him.

"The lord Woden, it seems, intends to do battle in his ceremonial robes!" chortled Osbern.

"His wedding gear, you mean! 'Twill be a bedraggled bridegroom who goes to meet his bride—if he lives!" said Cerdic tauntingly. "Do you not wish to don more suitable gear, lord of the raven?"

"Let him be, Cerdic," laughed Osbern. "Do not bait the fellow! His chieftainship will be brief and his wedding non-existent—let him enjoy the trappings of chieftainship whilst he may!"

"Do you wish for time in which to don more suitable attire, my lord?" enquired Siferth courteously.

"Nay, my lord, that will not be necessary," Woden replied composedly, turning to face Cerdic and waiting for him to make the first move.

Spear in hand, Cerdic advanced towards Woden, whilst Woden stood calm and relaxed, eyeing him soberly. Cerdic poised the spear, took careful aim and then threw the spear, and it hurtled through the air straight towards Woden.

It was within a few inches of Woden's chest when he leapt into action. He turned swiftly to the left and at right angles to the oncoming spear, so that it missed him by a hair's breadth, and he put out his right hand and seized it in its flight.

There were gasps of amazement from the onlookers at this feat, followed by an enthusiastic burst of applause which made Cerdic scowl with fury. Woden then poised the spear, and himself took careful aim, not, as was clearly expected, at his opponent, but high into the air where the spear hurtled over the heads of the spectators and then, like a boomerang, took a backward direction towards its thrower, finally falling to earth with a clatter at Woden's feet.

Cerdic, angered by the ovation given to Woden and by the obvious partisanship of the excited spectators, quickly pulled his battle-axe from his waist-belt and advanced menacingly towards his opponent.

Woden backed away this time, as if fearful of the attack. He continued to back, and Cerdic to advance, Cerdic grinning malevolently now, as if he derived enjoyment from tantalizing his adversary before making his attack.

But then Woden's back came up against the tall wooden pillar that supported the invasion bell, the bell which, when struck three times by the massive hammer beside it, gave warning to the Angles of an approaching enemy. Unable to move back any further, Woden stood and enigmatically faced his enemy.

The spectators gasped with anxiety for their newly-elected chieftain. Was he unprepared for Cerdic's skill and cunning? they asked themselves. Could an unarmed man, however courageous, combat an opponent armed to the teeth with sword, spear and battle-axe? Why does he not admit defeat before his skull is cleft in two?

Cerdic advanced to within striking distance of Woden.

"So, lord of the raven, you fight with your back to the wall!" he cried mockingly. "But I am a generous man. I have no desire to kill an unarmed adversary, albeit he is thus by his own choice. Renounce the chieftainship, lord of the raven, and Cerdic will let you live."

Woden said nothing. His eyes remained fixed on Cerdic, sizing him up and judging the instant when Cerdic would deliver the fateful blow.

Goaded into action by Woden's silence, Cerdic swung his battle-axe and lowered it with devastating force above the head of his victim. But in that split second before the battle-axe struck Woden's skull, an instant of time which was too fast to be seen by the naked eye, Woden leapt aside. The battle-axe landed on the wooden post, splitting it asunder for the top twelve inches and embedding itself in the wood, and causing the invasion bell to toll resoundingly as if in vociferous protest.

There were tumultuous cheers from the spectators at this stage, and deepening scowls and curses from the surprised and enraged Cerdic whose chagrin was increased by the arrival of a further crowd of people, who had been summoned thither in some alarm by the ringing of the bell.

Woden remained silent, his gaze as before never leaving that of his opponent, his expression betraying neither triumph nor anxiety, as he stooped to retrieve Cerdic's spear, which he then held in his left hand.

His shield protecting his body, Cerdic drew his sword and advanced towards Woden, who made no attempt to defend himself with the spear. Cerdic struck viciously at Woden's right arm, but Woden leapt aside just in time to avoid the lethal blade. This situation, with Cerdic striking at Woden, and Woden adroitly dodging the savage blows, continued for several minutes, Cerdic's expertise as a swordsman seeming matched by Woden's almost miraculous precision and quick-sightedness.

The excitement of the spectators had now grown to fever pitch and there were shouts of enthusiasm and admiration for Woden from all sides.

But then it happened.

The enthusiastic cries instantly gave way to cries of dismay as, nimbly avoiding a particularly vicious cut from Cerdic's sword, Woden tripped and fell headlong, to sprawl helplessly at the feet of his adversary.

With an exultant grin, Cerdic leapt forward and pressed the point of his sword against Woden's throat.

"The gods have spoken!" he exclaimed triumphantly.

"Do you accept me as your master, lord of the raven?"

Woden made no answer.

Cerdic pressed the point of his sword into Woden's throat, pricking the skin and drawing blood.

"Speak, lord of the raven!" growled Cerdic. "Do you accept me as your master?"

Still Woden made no answer.

"You shall accept me as your master before you die," declared Cerdic, enraged by Woden's silence. "You will beg me for the kindness of death but, before I grant you that mercy, you will acknowledge me as your master and the rightful chieftain of the Angles."

"That I shall never do," Woden said quietly.

"Then be warned, lord of the raven!" said Cerdic. "First I shall lop off each of your fingers, then each of your hands, then each of your feet, and then your privy parts—thus will I continue till you have acknowledged me your master."

"That I shall never do," Woden said, quietly as before.

"Then we will start with your left hand, the hand in which you hold the spear you scorned to use," Cerdic said malevolently.

He placed a heavy booted foot on Woden's left forearm, pressing it down until he had stopped the blood supply to Woden's hand and thus forced Woden's numbed fingers to relinquish the spear. Then he raised his sword, preparatory to cutting off the first of Woden's fingers. He held the sword poised a few inches above Woden's hand, watching his victim shrewdly and keeping the now-silent spectators in an agony of suspense.

But then, out of the corner of his eye, Cerdic saw something move. The spear? he thought. 'Tis impossible, but the spear appears to be moving of its own volition. He momentarily removed his gaze from his silent victim, and gave an involuntary start of horror.

The spear was no longer a spear. Of the same length as a spear, its head shaped like a spear's point, it was neverthe-less not a spear. It was a snake. Green and spotted, it was a snake of a type well known to huntsmen, for it was ofttimes found in the darkest depths of the forest and its venom was said to kill the strongest man or horse in the space of one minute.

Transfixed by fear, by this manifestation of evil, Cerdic was quite unable to strike the reptile with his sword. He stepped back in horror, tripped over the feet of his fallen adversary, lost his grip on both sword and shield, and fell headlong into the path of the steadily-advancing snake.

"Blood of Tiw!" he gasped in terror. "This is Loki's work!"

Woden leapt to his feet. "Loki's work, Cerdic, or the work of the sky gods? Acknowledge this as a sign from the gods, accept me as your chieftain, and I will kill the snake," he said dispassionately.

" 'Tis too late! And you have no sword," groaned Cerdic. "The creature is about to strike. I must remain perfectly still. If you take one step nearer or try to take my sword, 'twill be all up with me! May the gods forgive me, I recognise the truth too late—I did not see the hand of the gods in all that has happened."

"By invoking the gods you have saved your life, Cerdic," Woden told him.

Stepping swiftly between the terrified man and the snake, Woden struck the snake, giving it nine light and evenly-spaced chops along its length with the side of his hand. At once the snake ceased to move, and the onlookers who were now crowding forward to get a closer view of Woden's action, saw that the object of Cerdic's terror was now neither snake nor spear. In place of the mysterious object, lay nine glory twigs.

"Will you now pledge me your allegiance, my lord Cerdic?" asked Woden courteously.

"I will indeed, my lord," Cerdic said, getting to his feet and gazing at Woden in wonderment. "I am indebted to you for my life, and henceforth my life shall be dedicated to your service."

"Then, my lord Cerdic, I ask that you hand me the glory twigs one by one, as tokens of your allegiance," Woden said gravely.

A trifle hesitantly, as if he feared they might resume the likeness of a snake, Cerdic stooped and, picking up one of the twigs, presented it to Woden.

Woden accepted it graciously and then held it aloft that all those present might see it. It was no longer a glory twig: it was a shining gold goblet.

His hand shaking noticeably at this further manifestation of the power of the sky gods, Cerdic presented another glory twig to Woden, which was promptly transformed into a gold bracelet. This, passed around and tested for weight among those spectators nearest to Woden, was found to be of a type customarily used as a bracer to strengthen the wrist of a warrior wielding heavy weapons and was judged to weigh sixteen ounces of gold.

The procedure continued until Cerdic had presented all the glory twigs to Woden, by which time Woden was the possessor, not only of the goblet and bracelet, but of another similar bracelet, two gold rings, a gold helmet, a jewelled shoulder clasp, and two gold buckles. The gods, it seemed to the overawed spectators, had shown Woden an additional sign of their favour and approval of his chieftainship, by fitting him out with nine articles of a chieftain's regalia.

Woden held out one of the gold rings to Cerdic.

"Let this be a token between us, my lord," he said, placing the ring on the third finger of Cerdic's right hand. "You are a skilful and courageous warrior from all accounts. Use your courage and skill for good purpose. You have a strong will. Use that also for good purpose. You have shown resentment of my having been accepted as chieftain in preference to yourself. That is understandable. You are jealous of my having won the heart of the lady Ricole, in preference to yourself. That too is understandable. I have been sent here by the sky gods for a purpose. Your courage and skill as a warrior can aid me, if you will it, in that purpose. Can you, my lord Cerdic, subdue your natural resentment and jealousy sufficiently to take on the duties of leader of my *hearth-horde*?"

"Loki's bones!" exclaimed Cerdic in astonishment. "Are you serious, my lord?"

"I was never more serious."

"You are suggesting that I, your enemy, the one who would have killed you, tortured you to death, but for the intervention of the gods, should become the leader of your *hearth-horde*?" asked Cerdic incredulously.

"I am, my lord Cerdic."

"But why, my lord?" Cerdic asked uneasily, as if he suspected Woden of having some ulterior motive. "Why should you show me, of all people, such a mark of favour? Why should you trust me to lead your bodyguard, to be the protector of your left arm?"

"The gods in their wisdom have shown me the worse side, the evil side, of your nature, my lord," Woden explained. "They have yet to show me your better side."

"You believe there is a better side, my lord?" asked Cerdic, as if even he had doubt of it.

"Had the sky gods not known that you have a better side, they would have left you to the venom of the snake. . . ."

"But surely, my lord, it was you, not the sky gods, who saved me."

Woden ignored the interruption. "Know your enemy. That is the first precept of knowledge, Cerdic. I have known my enemy: I have not underrated him and am therefore in a position to ask that he becomes my friend. If the Angles are to become a great people, greater even than in Earl Leofgar's time, there is no room for an enemy within our gates. We must think as one man, offer allegiance to one leader. We must become a united people. As a united people we shall conquer; as a divided people we shall fall to the first of our foes, be they Saxon or Jute, who seek their fortunes upon our shore. What say you, Cerdic? Are you friend or enemy? Will you accept the leadership of my *hearth-horde*?"

"My lord, I cannot refuse you," Cerdic said whole-heartedly. "You are right in all that you have said. I know now that your wisdom and courage are such that no man in Angel could gainsay your right to be chieftain."

There were enthusiastic cheers from the spectators at this point and, in a sudden access of emotion, Cerdic fell to his knees before Woden and, in token of his duty as leader of the *hearth-horde* to guard his lord's left side, the side theoretically unprotected by his own sword, he grasped Woden's left hand in both of his own.

"Earl Woden," he said, thereby proclaiming his accept-ance of Woden as his chieftain, "I am honoured to accept the leadership of your *hearth-horde* and swear to be ever loyal and true to you, my lord."

"Thank you, Cerdic," Woden said quietly. "You will not regret so doing."

TWELVE

Whilst the contest between Woden and Cerdic had been taking place, Ricole had remained alone and apprehensive in the living chamber of the chieftain's dwelling which, if he survived the contest, would be Woden's home, just as it had formerly been Leofgar's home.

Ricole tried to close her ears to the sounds which emanated from the square. But it was no use. Try as she did to think only joyful thoughts as Woden had bidden her, she found her attention caught by the mixture of sounds: by shouts of encouragement, consternation, disappointment, excitement and jubilation. But disappointment for whom? she asked herself. For Woden or for Cerdic? Jubilation for whom? For Cerdic or for Woden?

Am I to lose my beloved lord after all? she wondered miserably. Was he given back to me only to be snatched away from me again? I am not yet his wife according to the laws of the Angles. Should Woden die and I am found to be carrying a bastard, I well know what my fate will be. Virginity is prized, and fornication, except with slaves, is forbidden amongst our people, and I would kill myself and my child rather than be subjected to the punishment prescribed for such a transgression.

Why, Ricole asked herself, did I give myself to Woden last night? Why did I not insist that we waited until after our bridal? Ricole sighed, and then smiled gently. Given the choice, would I not act in the same way again? she asked herself. My love for Woden is such that I could deny him nothing. My joy and happiness are inextricably bound up with his joy and happiness. His future is my future. If he has no future, if he meets his death at Cerdic's hands as he may well do since the odds are heavily against him, then I too shall have no future, for I would not wish to live without him. If he dies. . . .

Cerdic is a ruthless adversary and a skilful warrior, and is fully armed. How could any unarmed man be a match for him? Holy Freya, protect the man I love, I beseech you, and bring him out of the encounter unscathed!

She heard the entrance door of the dwelling being opened and she heard the voices of her servants. Then she heard purposeful male footsteps approaching the chamber. Her heart thumped suffocatingly in her breast, as she waited in fear and apprehension. Was it Woden himself, or was it one of her kinsmen, a triumphant Cerdic perchance, coming to inform her that Woden was dead?

The door of the living chamber was quietly opened and Ricole looked up in alarm, to see Woden standing in the doorway smiling at her.

She dissolved into tears.

Woden came in, closed the door, and enfolded her in his arms.

"Why so sad, little one? Did you hope to see Cerdic standing in the doorway?" he asked teasingly.

"Alas, I feared greatly for you, my lord," Ricole wept. "Unarmed as you were, it seemed that Cerdic must overcome you, and I weep tears of relief that you are safe."

"You thought that Cerdic would kill me?" Woden asked, incredulously.

Ricole nodded mutely, clinging to him as if she feared he would disappear before her very eyes.

"You thought foolishly, little one," Woden said chidingly. "Did I not promise you that all would be well? You deserve to be beaten for doubting the word of your lord."

"You are not my husband yet," Ricole reminded him, a trifle on her mettle.

"I am your chieftain," Woden said, kissing her lovingly. "As such, I expect obedience. You thought foolishly in imagining that Cerdic would kill me—Cerdic is the leader of my *hearth-horde*."

"The leader of your *hearth-horde*?" asked Ricole incredulously. "You are teasing me again, my lord, and you are cruel and heartless to treat me so when I have been tormented by anxiety for you. Cerdic is your enemy."

"Cerdic *was* my enemy," corrected Woden. "He is now the leader of my *hearth-horde*."

"You are serious, my lord?"

"Curious that! It must run in your family," said Woden infuriatingly.

"What must run in my family?" asked Ricole defensively.

"Cerdic asked me that same question when I offered him the leadership of my *hearth-horde*. 'Are you serious, my lord?' he asked."

"My lord, I do not understand what has befallen, but praise be to Freya you are unharmed," Ricole said, standing back to survey him critically. "Your ceremonial robes are quite unmarked. Perchance the contest has not yet taken place or it has been postponed until the morrow. *Ja*, that must surely be the answer. Or perchance Cerdic has chosen to find a less conspicuous means of killing you, because he fears to displease the Witan."

"We fought and I won—on points," Woden said shortly. "And Cerdic afterwards pledged me his allegiance."

"Do not trust him, my lord, I beg you," Ricole said in renewed alarm. "He is my own kinsman but I know him to be untrustworthy."

"Henceforth Cerdic will be a changed man," Woden said with conviction. "Whatever his faults, he will be loyal and true to me. The gods have made that plain."

"And what of Osbern?" Ricole asked. "He has an even greater claim to the chieftainship than Cerdic. Do you expect Osbern also to be loyal and true?"

"Osbern, alas, is a different matter," Woden said quietly. "He has yet to acknowledge me as his chieftain. Osbern, I admit, will need careful watching if he is not to bring the Angles to disaster. But the wishes of the gods will prevail in the end."

"But if. . . ."

"That is my last word on the subject, my lady," Woden said, kissing her again. "I did not come here to discuss such trivia. . . ."

"Trivia!" exclaimed Ricole indignantly. "You call. . . ."

". . . I came to tell you that our bridal will take place in half an hour. The chief priest and people are already assembling in the temple, for the wedding of a chieftain is a spectacle none will willingly forgo. In half an hour, my lady, your handmaidens shall escort you to the temple and I shall be awaiting you there."

"In half an hour? What if I am not ready, my lord?"

"You will be ready."

"But my eyes are red with weeping," Ricole said, dabbing at her tear-stained face with a lace-edged handkerchief. "Would you wish our people to think you have a reluctant bride, my lord?"

"In half an hour's time you will stand beside me in the temple, serene and beautiful as ever, and become my wife," Woden told her. "Till then, my lady, I bid you farewell."

Before Ricole could make further protest, Woden had turned determinedly away and was making rapidly for the doorway.

As she watched him go, Ricole's mind was a mixture of emotions. My lord's strong will brooks no refusal, she thought. Despite his undoubted love for me, he is still a stranger. I believe his love for me surpasses all other influences—but one. What is his secret? It is clear that he is controlled by some mysterious power. But what power? Whatever it is, Woden dwells always within its shadow. It is part of him and can at times, as during his hanging on the tree, control him totally. At such times, his love for me could well be overruled. That I must accept.

But then the sombre moments passed and Ricole forgot her doubts. Suddenly her heart was singing with joy, her lips were curved into a radiant smile, and the tears that still hovered on her eyelashes became tears of happiness. She was a bride going forth to meet her bridegroom. She was a woman going to meet her lover. She was loved and beloved. What more can I ask of the gods? she thought. Am I not about to become the bride of Woden, lord of the raven, chieftain of the Angles? Am I not the most fortunate woman in the whole world?

She called for Ceolburh and together they put the finishing touches to her bridal array.

THIRTEEN

Accompanied by four handmaidens, Ricole arrived at the entrance to the temple at the appointed time, and at once Woden, with Cerdic standing beside him, came forward to greet her.

Woden took her hand and led her inside the crowded temple, where they stood side by side in front of the statue of Freya while the marriage ceremony took place. Freya's serene gaze seemed fixed on the bride and bridegroom in loving compassion but, despite the beautiful face and accustomed as she was to the statue, Ricole was conscious as never before of the gross, exaggeratedly pregnant body of the goddess. Will my body look like that in a few months' time? thought Ricole. Will my lord still love me if I look like that? Alas, I am allowing my thoughts to wander, which ill-becomes a bride on her wedding day. I must give all my attention to the words of the priest.

She glanced at Woden a trifle guiltily: he caught her glance and turned to smile gently at her as if he understood her thoughts, and Ricole blushed and demurely lowered her eyes in a manner befitting a bride.

"Look graciously we entreat thee, holy goddess, upon this man and this maiden and further thy own desire for the continuance of mankind," intoned the priest. "Let the union of these two, blessed and protected by thy divine assistance, be joyous and fruitful."

At this point, Woden placed a gold ring on the salver

which stood on the altar and the ring was blessed by the priest.

"Holy goddess, bless this ring which I am blessing in thy name," said the priest, "to the end that she who is to wear it may be wholly faithful to her husband. So may she abide in thy peace and in accordance with thy will, living always in love given and returned: through Freya our mother, amen."

The priest next sprinkled the ring with holy water drawn from the holy well in the Sacred Grove, and gave the ring to Woden.

Woden turned to Ricole and took her left hand in his.

"With this ring I thee wed, with my body I thee worship, and with all my earthly goods I thee endow," he said.

He then placed the ring on Ricole's thumb, saying: "In the name of Allfather, oldest and wisest of the gods, second lord of Armies, third lord of the Spear, fourth Smiter, fifth All-knowing, sixth Fulfiller-of-wishes, seventh Farspoken, eighth Shaker, ninth Burner, tenth Destroyer, eleventh Protector, and twelfth Gelding. . . ."

Then on her forefinger, saying: "and in the name of Freya, goddess of love and fertility. . . ."

Then on her middle finger, saying: "and in the name of our mighty protectors, the sky gods. . . ."

And, lastly, on her third finger where he left the ring.

The priest addressed the bride and bridegroom.

"Go now, children of Freya, mother of us all. Go and bring forth in Earth's embrace," he said.

*   *   *

That night, alone in her bridal bower, waiting for the arrival of her bridegroom, Ricole was overcome by nervousness. She was conscious as never before that until ten days

ago Woden had been an unknown stranger. There was still
so much she did not know about him. He had come to
Angel as a stranger in a mysterious ship. He had spoken
scarcely at all of his past life, if indeed he remembered it.
Whence had he come? Since his arrival, he had miraculously
survived a cruel death, had been the victor in an unequal
combat, and had, so he believed, begotten a child on her.

As the bride and bridegroom had left the temple after
their wedding, the heart-warming cheers and congratulations of their people ringing in their ears, Ricole had suddenly felt as if she were married to a stranger. All through
the marriage feast which had followed, she had remained
quiet and pensive, feeling separated from the gaiety around
her, and now, alone in the bower, she was nervous and
apprehensive.

The bower, formerly Earl Leofgar's bower, had lovingly
been converted into a bridal bower by Ricole's handmaidens.
A log fire burned brightly in the hearth and filled the
chamber with warmth and light, small posies of spring
flowers had been tied to the sides of the bed with ribbons,
and garlands of flowers and fragrant herbs decorated the
wooden walls. The bed had been sumptuously furnished
with plump cushions covered in finely-embroidered wool,
and was draped with the white fur coverlet which Ricole
had first seen in the cave and which Woden had brought
with him to Angel.

Her handmaidens had helped Ricole disrobe, had bathed
and perfumed her body with oil of musk, brushed her
blonde hair into a shining cascade, and dressed her in a
white bedgown which, despite its simplicity, its shapeless-
ness and long flowing sleeves, was low-cut in the bodice
and displayed rather than obscured her charms.

With secret reluctance, Ricole had then dismissed her
handmaidens who had departed giggling from the chamber,

and had seated herself on a wooden stool in front of the flower-decorated mirror of polished bronze which hung on the wall. In an effort to still her trembling hands, she picked up her hairbrush and again brushed her already-shining hair.

Woden quietly came into the bower, closed the door, and stood watching her from the doorway.

"Your handmaidens told me you were ready for me, my lady," he said formally.

Ricole continued brushing her hair, keeping up a pretence, as if his arrival were a little premature.

"I am almost ready, my lord," she said absently.

"Your hair needs further brushing? In truth I believe that no amount of brushing could add greater beauty to your tresses," Woden said, taking the hairbrush from her and, a trifle inexpertly, starting to brush her hair. "Is something troubling you, beloved?"

"My lord, this is our bridal night and yet already. . . ." Ricole paused. Is that the real reason why I am troubled? she wondered. Is it not because I suddenly see my bridegroom as a stranger?

"And yet already you are mine," Woden finished for her. "And that causes you concern."

"It would have caused my lord father concern."

"Your lord father once took that which was not lawfully his—for the benefit of his people. I have done likewise. Your father and I have much in common," Woden told her.

"What do you mean, my lord?" Ricole asked, a little coldly.

"Your father once took a man's life for the good of the Anglian people," Woden explained. "I have given a man life for the good of the Anglian people."

"Our child, you mean?" asked Ricole shyly.

"Of course. And yet you are beset by guilt. Is it better then to take than to give? Is it better to hate than to love?"

"My father did not hate Olaf—he was his brother," protested Ricole. "He did what he did for the good of our people."

Woden looked thoughtful and put down the hair brush. "I wonder! Could your father have murdered Olaf if he had not hated him? Is it possible to cold-bloodedly kill a person one loves? I think not, little one," he said gently.

Ricole sighed. "Alas, my lord, I confess I know not the answer to your questions. Your wisdom is great and you confuse me with such talk, so that. . . ."

"So that you forget your doubts and remember only our love?" Woden asked, smilingly.

"I was a little nervous, my lord," Ricole admitted.

"Of me?"

"Of whom else? You suddenly seemed like a stranger, my lord."

"I was a stranger until ten days ago—now I am your husband and the father of your child."

"But. . . ."

Woden stood behind her and, watching her expression carefully in the mirror, drew down the flimsy bodice of her bedgown and exposed the voluptuous beauty of her breasts. He placed gentle caressing fingers on her nipples.

"You are telling me you do not want me?" he asked in a low voice. "I will leave our bridal bower now if you wish it."

"Where would you go, my lord?" Ricole asked in breathless alarm, her excitement transcending all else as he touched her.

"To seek for another woman with hair like yours and breasts like yours," he said coolly.

"You really would?" Ricole asked, anxiously.

Woden nodded, his eyes twinkling. "*Ja*, I should seek, as I said, but I should not find. There is no other woman as beautiful and as desirable as you, little one," he said.

Awakened by his caresses, her body aflame with desire, Ricole turned and threw herself into his arms.

"Oh, my lord, I beg you forgive my doubts!" she exclaimed passionately. "I love you so much, much more than I can say. You are here and you are mine. Take me, my lord—take me now!"

"Take you where?" he asked tantalisingly, lifting her up in strong arms nonetheless.

"To our bed, where else?" she cried passionately. "Take me, my lord, and love me over and over again."

FOURTEEN

The Angles, like all Norsemen, were, by tradition, fierce independent fighting men who lived by seafaring and agricultural skills. During the summer months, they journeyed to other shores where they raided the burghs of enemy tribes, killing all who stood in their path, and plundering cattle, slaves, and treasure-chests of silver and gold.

They loved fighting, for battle, like the sea and the storm, was in their blood. Storm and gale offered them a challenge, stimulating their muscles and their minds. Did not the thunder-bolts and lightning give them energy? Faced with danger, from man or element, they whole-heartedly accepted the challenge, giving no mercy and asking no mercy.

Their only loyalty, their all-consuming loyalty, was to their lord and to their kin. From their lord, the warriors customarily received their shelter, their food and their ale. From him they received their coats of ringed mail, their runed swords, gold and silver bracelets for their adornment, and ring money. They followed him into battle in the summer months, and feasted and sang and slept round his hearth in winter. For their lord and their kin they lived; for their lord and their kin, if necessary, they would die. Such had been the unwritten law of the Angles from time immemorial.

The burgh of Angel, situated about a quarter of a mile from the shore, had been built on the edge of a great forest. Over the years, vast areas of this forest had been cleared with the aid of iron axes, and ploughs drawn by teams of oxen, thus making holdings for the farmers and providing two great communal fields. Beyond the fields was the common pasture where the farmers kept their sheep and cattle.

The numberless tribes of Denmark, Frisia, Jutland, and Saxony, battled unceasingly for survival or supremacy. Many of the smaller, weaker tribes had been overrun by the stronger ones over the years, and had been forced to pay allegiance to the chieftains of their erstwhile enemies, becoming integrated with the stronger tribe as a consequence. This had looked like being the fate of the Angles for, during the latter months of Leofgar's leadership, with his own once formidable strength gone, and lacking sons to aid him, the Angles' power had been alarmingly weakened, until their foremost concern had been survival.

It therefore became Woden's first duty as chieftain to reverse this process. His supreme task was to increase the strength and power of the Angles, until they could again take their place amongst the foremost tribes.

During the weeks which followed Woden's election, under his guidance and leadership, the life of the tribe began to resume a normal pattern. Knowing themselves protected from marauders, the farmers devoted their attention to the all-important tasks of tilling their fields and tending their herds.

The warriors were subjected to a rigorous training programme, in order to increase their proficiency in the skills of war. Woden selected leaders who would each be in charge of nine men, and the mornings were given over solely to battle practice, at which Woden himself was always present, advising, criticising, encouraging and teaching. Their chieftain, the warriors were quick to discover, whilst he personally fought only with a spear, was an expert with sword and battle-axe, and he lost little time in imparting his expertness to his men.

Despite Cerdic's whole-hearted capitulation to Woden, Osbern had still not given his allegiance to the new chieftain. Not in his heart, that is. Ostensibly he had done so. He had knelt before Woden, had placed his hand on Woden's spear, and had vowed fealty and homage, as had all his kinsmen. Having witnessed Cerdic's unexpected defeat in the contest, Osbern had decided that he himself must employ other means than open combat to achieve his aim. He must lull his enemy, for he secretly regarded Woden as such, into a false sense of security, and formulate a plan which would destroy Woden and present him, Osbern, with the chieftainship.

All of his kinsmen having pledged their allegiance to Woden, Osbern knew he could expect no support from the Angles, except from his own hired henchmen. He must therefore seek help from outside. Where shall I obtain better help, he asked himself, than in the domain of the Angles' traditional enemies the Saxons, the nearest tribe of whom, the Haewards, dwell many miles to the south?

Having let it be known at Angel that he was going on a week's hunting expedition in the depths of the forest, accompanied by his henchmen, Osbern one day presented himself at the gates of the Saxon burgh and asked to be taken to Earl Seaxwulf, the Haeward chieftain.

"What brings you here, my lord Osbern?" asked Seaxwulf suspiciously as he received Osbern's humble obeisance.

"Since Earl Leofgar's death, of which you have doubtless been informed, my lord, my people have elected a new chieftain, one by the name of Woden," Osbern said.

"Whence came this new chieftain?" Seaxwulf asked. "He is not of the Angles, I understand."

"None knows whence he came, my lord."

"I confess it surprises me, my lord Osbern, that the Angles should elect a stranger as their new chieftain."

"He won the confidence of the Witan and the more gullible of our people by trickery, my lord," Osbern explained. "Inspired no doubt by Loki, the Evil One, he allowed himself to be hung on a tree in the Sacred Grove for nine nights, whereupon he died and returned to life. Instead of recognising the trick for what it was—Loki's handiwork—the Angles saw it as a sign that the gods favoured Woden."

"And you think they are mistaken?"

"I am sure they are mistaken, my lord," Osbern said earnestly. "Woden used another trick to further his own designs. He violated the lady Ricole, Earl Leofgar's daughter, and afterwards forced her to marry him. He boasts he has begotten a son on the lady Ricole, a son who will be Earl Leofgar's grandson. Loving Earl Leofgar as they did, my people were influenced by this and promptly elected Woden as chieftain."

"Have all Earl Leofgar's thanes and warriors vowed allegiance to this man?" asked Seaxwulf.

"*Ja*, my lord."

"Excepting yourself, of course."

Osbern hesitated. "I also vowed allegiance to Woden. I had no choice, my lord. In truth I regard myself as the only rightful chieftain, as Earl Leofgar stole the chieftainship from my father," he said, a trifle defensively.

"Ah!" exclaimed Seaxwulf, nodding his head shrewdly. "I begin to understand your reason for coming to me. You claim you had no choice than to give allegiance to Woden? A man of honour always has a choice, my lord. You could have challenged the miracle-worker to a contest of arms. As the conqueror of such a man, you would have won glory and renown."

"Woden deals in witchcraft and sorcery, my lord," Osbern explained. "The lord Cerdic, nephew of Earl Leofgar, who himself claims the chieftainship, challenged Woden to open combat. Cerdic was beaten, again by trickery. If one is to thwart the Loki-inspired power of Woden, one must resort to more devious means."

"You have a plan?" asked Seaxwulf. "Of course you have, or you would not have come here to the stronghold of your traditional enemies. You want something from me, my lord Osbern—tell me of it."

"My lord, the power of the Angles diminished greatly during the latter months of Earl Leofgar's rule. . . ."

"Not greatly enough for our raids on Angel to meet with any notable success," Seaxwulf interposed grimly.

"Although during these first weeks of Woden's rule, the tribe appears to have returned to a settled state, I believe there is much unrest beneath the surface," continued Osbern. "I believe that a formidable Saxon force, a concerted attack on Angel, would be victorious at the present time."

"If Woden is the man you say he is, he will not easily be vanquished," Seaxwulf pointed out.

"Faced with a formidable force, I believe the Angles would lay down their arms. I believe that allegiance to Woden is not deeply rooted but rests on fear and superstition. The lord Cerdic paid lip service to Woden after he was defeated but he covets the lady Ricole and will, I am certain, let pass no opportunity of ousting Woden and winning the lady Ricole for himself."

"The lord Cerdic, you say, covets both the chieftainship and the lady Ricole," Seaxwulf said. "Should we take Angel and kill Earl Woden, will not Cerdic also become a thorn in your flesh?"

"Cerdic must die," Osbern said uncompromisingly. "Like

Woden himself, he must be slain by Saxon warriors. Once he has served his purpose, has deserted Woden who curiously seems to trust him implicitly, Cerdic must die—he has no right to the chieftainship, and the lady Ricole shall be mine."

"Should I agree to your plan, and I admit it has much to recommend it, am I to understand that, when we attack Angel, you would seek to provoke panic and dismay amongst the Anglian warriors?" Seaxwulf enquired, shrewdly. "You believe that they will fall into disarray, will lay down their arms and surrender?"

"As a member of Woden's *hearth-horde*, I shall at first make pretence of following our lord," Osbern explained. "But then, at the auspicious moment, as your warriors are advancing towards us, I shall slip from the ranks and shall cry out: 'The stranger has betrayed us! He to whom we vowed allegiance, who appeared so mysteriously from the sea, is naught but a Saxon adventurer. We are betrayed! There is no hope for us. Throw down your arms, warriors of Angel, or 'tis certain not a man among us will live to tell of the betrayal. But before you do so, kill the betrayer, the enemy within our gates!'"

"You are convinced they will hearken to you?" asked Seaxwulf impassively, watching his visitor shrewdly.

"My people are bewitched by the stranger from the sea, my lord," Osbern answered bitterly. "They are blind to the truth, for they fail to see the Evil One who lurks within their very walls. But once they see a formidable Saxon force approaching our shores, and they hear my voice telling them that Woden has betrayed us, then the scales will fall from their eyes and they will turn to me in their fear of the unknown."

"And if all comes to pass as you say, my lord Osbern— what then?" asked Seaxwulf. "What, apart from the lady

Ricole, do you hope to gain from turning traitor to your people?"

"I am no traitor, my lord!" exclaimed Osbern indignantly. "I but seek to rescue my people from the machinations of an upstart, a ravisher of virgins, a creature whose evil power presages nothing but disaster for the Angles."

"I ask you again, my lord Osbern," Seaxwulf persisted. "What advantage do you seek for yourself?"

"Once Woden is dead and the Angles are defeated, they would become vassals and would vow fealty and homage to you, my lord Seaxwulf," Osbern explained, uneasily aware of the Saxon chieftain's penetrating gaze. "I should expect to be appointed as acting chieftain and, as such, would accept you as my overlord. I should then take the lady Ricole to wife."

For a few moments there was silence in the chamber as Seaxwulf gave thought to the matter, gazing unwaveringly at Osbern meanwhile as if he sought to read his mind.

He and Osbern each had his own interests at heart.

Seaxwulf thought: Does the man think me a fool? Does he think that I, too, am a man of dishonour? A man who plays traitor to his lord and his kin, is a creature beyond contempt. He can be trusted by none. Such a one forfeits the right to live. All the same, his plan has much to recommend it. If, with his assistance, I defeat the Angles, I shall then dispose of him and place a Saxon in command at Angel. *Ja*, the lord Osbern could well be a useful tool in achieving my long-standing ambition—conquest of the Angles.

Osbern thought: Does the man think me a fool? Does he think I am a man of dishonour? A man who plays traitor to his lord and his kin is a creature beyond contempt. He can be trusted by none. Does he truly believe I am such a one? All the same, the plan has much to recommend it. If, with my assistance, the Saxons defeat the Angles, once I am chieftain, I shall use every possible means to rebuild the tribe and throw off the Saxon yoke. *Ja*, the lord Seaxwulf could be a very useful tool in achieving my long-standing ambition—the chieftainship of the Angles.

FIFTEEN

When a messenger, breathing heavily from exertion, brought news of the Saxon invasion, Woden was seated in the Heorot engaged in earnest discussion with Cerdic and Oswy.

"The Saxons, my lord!" gasped out the messenger. "Saxons are approaching our shores!"

The three men leapt to their feet.

"You are certain of this?" Woden asked the messenger, sternly. "This is not another false alarm like the two ship-wrecked fishing boats that were washed up on the shore yesterday?"

"The look-out men have sighted a fleet of vessels heading towards Angel, my lord," the messenger insisted. "All carry the Wolf emblem of the Haeward tribe of the Saxons. My lord Siferth was there on the shore and sent me to warn you whilst he hastened to the square to sound the invasion bell."

As if to corroborate the messenger's words, the tolling of the invasion bell fell mournfully on the ears of Woden and the two warriors.

"Doubtless, having heard of Earl Leofgar's death and that we were ten days without a new chieftain, the Saxons hope to surprise us in a state of chaos, my lord," Cerdic said grimly. "They expect us to be disorganised and unprepared for attack—the Haewards are the most northernly of the Saxon tribes and have ever been our nearest and most for-midable enemies."

"Then they are in for a disappointment," Woden said calmly, making swiftly for the armoury, the chamber which adjoined the Heorot and where he and his *hearth-horde* stored their battle harness.

He was closely followed by Cerdic and Oswy.

"Let us hope it is not a large force, my lord," said Oswy.

"How many vessels have been sighted?" Woden called out, to the messenger.

"The look-out counted five, my lord," the man replied. "My lord Siferth estimated that there were about five hundred men, a hundred to each ship."

"A sizeable body of men, my lord," Cerdic said in dismay. "'Tis clear the Saxons mean to overwhelm us and are sending a concentrated force to our shores."

"How many warriors have we here in Angel at the present time?" asked Oswy anxiously.

"About three hundred," Woden told him tightening the straps of his gold helmet and seizing his spear.

"Despite our vigorous training programme of the past weeks, we are still under-strength," said Cerdic gloomily, seizing his battle-axe and thrusting his sword into its hanger.

Without stopping to don further harness, pushing past the other members of the *hearth-horde* who had hurried to the armoury on hearing the invasion bell, Woden, accompanied by Cerdic and Oswy, made rapidly for the door.

All at Angel had heard the bell and already men were hurrying into the square outside the Heorot, men in varying stages of dress and undress, for none had stopped to don full battle array. They stood, chattering and laughing noisily to hide their underlying tension, awaiting Woden's arrival, each man wearing the wide leather belt from which his sword was suspended, and holding his shield in his left

E

hand and his battle-axe in his right.

It is to be hoped the gods are on our side this day, Cerdic thought as he joined his warriors, for we are not yet ready to meet so large a force. The men looked bewildered and uneasy despite their outward cheerfulness, as if already they have forgotten the discipline and training of the past weeks. Trust the Saxon devils to take advantage of our misfortune! Trust them to strike now when, so soon after Earl Leofgar's death, Earl Woden has had insufficient time to fully train the warriors.

Osbern joined Woden and Cerdic at that moment, his face expressing grave anxiety.

"My lord," he said, addressing Woden, "the Saxons have landed and are already advancing across the beach towards the burgh."

"How many are there?" Woden asked.

"A little over five hundred, my lord," Osbern said, corroborating Siferth's estimate.

Making no comment on this statement, Woden raised his spear, Gungnir, aloft.

"To the shore!" he cried.

Running swiftly, with Cerdic and his *hearth-horde* beside him and the other warriors following closely on their heels, Woden made for the shore.

Thus, seriously unprepared, the Angles came face to face with the fast-approaching Saxons.

Knowing the Saxons to be highly-trained, skilful warriors, Woden was in no doubt of the precariousness of the Angles' position. As Angles and Saxons came within sight of each other, his orders were firm and decisive.

Again he raised his spear high in the air with both hands, so that it caught the sun's rays and its dazzling brilliance became visible to all.

"Form a close-knit circle around me," he commanded,

"and then form a linden-wall with your shields."

Despite their astonishment, the men obeyed instantly, forming an immense close-knit circle, their hide-covered wooden shields overlapping each other and forming a protective wall.

"Advance on the enemy!" cried Woden from his position in the centre of the circle, holding his spear now in his right hand.

Under the firm commands and directions of their chieftain, the men behind the shield wall advanced slowly and inexorably, foot by foot, towards the enemy.

But then came an interruption.

Cerdic, standing in the circle between Osbern and Oswy, gaped in astonishment for a moment, unable at first to believe the evidence of his eyes and ears.

For Osbern had leapt forward from the circle—which was promptly ordered by Woden to close its ranks—had sprinted a short distance towards the oncoming Saxons, and was turning to face the oncoming Angles.

"Warriors of Angel, the stranger has betrayed us!" Osbern cried, resoundingly. "He to whom we vowed allegiance, who appeared mysteriously from the sea, is naught but a Saxon adventurer. We are betrayed! There is no hope for us. Throw down your arms, or 'tis certain not a man of us will live to tell of our betrayal. . . ."

But Osbern's words seemingly fell on deaf ears. The Angles continued to advance steadily towards the Saxons, and Osbern, still shouting, was forced to back away. Not a single man spoke to Osbern or attempted to break from the battle circle and, at last, realising his appeal had failed and that he was trapped between the two advancing forces, Osbern turned and fled.

Realising that his action would for ever make him an outcast from his people, Osbern took what seemed to be

the only course open to him if he were to preserve his life:
he fled towards the Saxon ships which, well guarded, had
been moored close in to the shore. Hoping to receive
sanctuary until the battle was concluded and the Angles
had been defeated as he still expected them to be, he made
to board one of the Saxon ships.

"What brings you here, Angle?" asked one of the guards
unpleasantly.

"I seek sanctuary, for I am the ally of your lord," Osbern
replied haughtily.

"Your name?"

"Osbern, son of Olaf."

"By Frigg! 'Tis Osbern, son of Olaf, mates," the guard
chortled, turning to his companions. "Did our lord not speak
of him?"

"He did, he certainly did, mate," agreed the other guards.

"Then make way for me, my good man," Osbern said,
trying in vain to hide his uneasiness.

"You shall get no sanctuary here, Anglian traitor," said
the guard.

"You have no right. . . ."

Osbern got no further. The guard's arm shot out and
dealt him a hefty blow on the chin which, taking him by
surprise, flung him backwards from the ship, and he landed
heavily on the wet sand. He looked up dazedly to see the
guard advancing towards him, battle-axe in hand.

"Spare me!" Osbern pleaded. "Do not kill me, I beg you.
I am your lord's ally."

"You are a traitor and our lord has no dealings with
traitors," the guard said savagely. "You are a traitor to
your lord and to your kin and, as such, death is too good
for you. I shall not kill you, Osbern, son of Olaf."

Osbern screamed with agony as the battle-axe struck him,
once on each of his legs, splintering his bones and reducing

his flesh to a bloody pulp. He saw with a cruel clarity the satisfied grin on the face of the guard, he saw his own blood dripping slowly from the battle-axe, and he saw the sudden reddening of the sand. I shall never walk again, was his last thought before he lost consciousness.

Meanwhile, the two opposing forces, Angle and Saxon, had conjoined. As they came within fighting distance of each other, the battle raged fast and furiously. Men fell on both sides, but any Saxon who ventured within range of the murderous battle-axes which swung this way and that above the shield wall, was immediately slain or severely wounded.

The great circle of shields had a demoralising effect upon the opposing Saxons. Superstitious to a degree, it seemed to them that they were no longer fighting men like themselves in equal combat. They were fighting a gigantic monster whose limbs were perfectly co-ordinated, a monster which moved under the command of the being who dwelt in its midst and issued commands as if inspired by some quite inhuman agency.

As the Angles advanced, killing or maiming all who lay in their path, the Saxons fell back under the onslaught towards the shore and their moored boats.

The guards in charge of the Saxon boats had watched the slow, reptilian advance of the Angles, and the retreat of their comrades, with dismay. Already their hands were busy with the mooring ropes, making ready for swift departure.

As, at Woden's command, the Angles broke from the circle and fell furiously upon the already depleted Saxons, Earl Seaxwulf gave the command for orderly retreat.

To the accompaniment of cheers and derisive shouts from the triumphant Angles, the remaining Saxons, numbering now only half those who had disembarked, jumped thankfully into their boats. The boats leapt into life and gathered way, assisted downstream by the falling tide and strong current, skimming through the waters of the estuary and making towards the open sea.

The victorious Angles lined the shore, brandishing their weapons menacingly at the departing Saxons, and whooping with joy and relief at having triumphed over the unequal odds. Their own losses had been minimal, despite the superior number of the enemy.

As the Saxons reached the mouth of the estuary and, turning southward, disappeared from view, the Angles turned to look with pride and admiration, not unmixed with awe, at their chieftain. Woden's expression was calm and practical as he started to give orders to Oswy for the disposal of the slain.

But the Angles had fought as one man. Now they would cheer as one man. They would leave no doubt of the strength of their devotion for their chieftain, the lord of the raven, the man who in a short space of time had become their hero.

"Wo . . . o . . . o . . . den! Wo . . . o . . . o . . . den!" they cried with one voice, in the same way as for centuries yet to come, their descendants, in times of danger or victory, would raise a cry to Woden.

Woden smilingly acknowledged the ovation which followed and then turned to speak to Oswy.

"See to it that the injured are carried up to the burgh and that the numbers of the slain are counted," he said practically. "Then make your report to me in the Heorot."

He turned, and with Cerdic beside him, started to make his way back to the burgh.

"My lord," Cerdic said, "there will be much to celebrate tonight, for our people rejoice and will long remember this victory."

"The men did well, Cerdic. I am proud of them," Woden answered warmly. "But we must not rest on our laurels. There is much work to be done before we have the formidable fighting force we need, before the Angles are spoken of with awe by our enemies, and with pride throughout the land of Denmark."

"After today, my lord, the name of Woden will surely be a byword among our enemies," Cerdic said, his hero-worship of his chieftain undisguised, "and an inspiration to our people."

SIXTEEN

The nature of the brutal warfare between the various Teutonic tribes, precluded the likelihood of a warrior surviving the battle with a serious injury. A skull cleft in two by a battle-axe caused instant death, as did a similar blow from a seax, the short sword favoured by the Saxons and whence derived their name. Men either survived the battle unscathed or with a superficial injury which was ignored, or they died on the battlefield.

The Saxon dead were left where they had fallen, as was customarily the treatment of an invading enemy. The scavengers and carrion birds, the hawks and crows, which always accompanied an invading fleet, went quickly about their business, feasting on the flesh until the bones were picked clean, after which the remains would be buried in a hastily-dug communal pit. The Anglian dead would be ritually cremated on a pyre that same evening.

"The wounded have been taken to one of the unused slave huts, my lord, and are being tended by the lady Ricole and her women," Oswy said later to Woden, when he went to the Heorot to make his report. "The wounded are few in number, but there are many Saxon dead."

"How many Saxons were slain?" asked Woden.

"More than two hundred, my lord."

"And what of our own casualties?"

"About twenty dead, my lord, and only one seriously injured."

"His name?" asked Woden, curtly.

"Osbern, son of Olaf," Cerdic said enigmatically.

"How was he injured?" enquired Woden, showing no surprise at this information. "He fled from the battle apparently unharmed."

"He says his legs were smashed by a Saxon battle-axe. Beyond that he refuses to speak of the matter. One thing is certain. Osbern will never walk again. He asks for you, my lord. I told him that our lord does not associate with traitors, but. . . ." Cerdic paused, as if reluctant to say more.

"And?"

"The lady Ricole insisted that I inform you of his request."

"I will see him," Woden said, and abruptly turned and left the Heorot, leaving Cerdic gazing after him in astonished disapproval.

Woden rapidly made his way to the wooden hut where the injured man lay, and he spoke briefly to Ricole before turning his attention to Osbern.

Lying on a straw mattress which was curtained off by a blanket from the mattresses of the Saxon injured, Osbern appeared to be asleep.

Ricole looked cool and efficient in a voluminous white apron. She had been trained from childhood, as were all noblewomen of her race, in nursing and healing, and in the use of herbal potions and medicaments. She had been trained to remain calm and practical in the face of the most ghastly injuries, neither to blanch nor shudder whatever the provocation, and to act as minor surgeon when necessary.

"How is Osbern?" Woden asked her.

"His legs are severely injured, my lord," Ricole answered softly. "He suffers great pain and even the infusion of poppy juice I have given him, does not give him ease for long. He begs for death."

Woden nodded grimly but made no comment. He stared down thoughtfully at the heavily drugged man.

Osbern's battle harness had been removed and he lay naked under the coarsely woven woollen blankets. His eyes were closed and sunken, and blood oozed from his lower lip where he had bitten it against the pain.

"Already the effects of the infusion are wearing off," Ricole said concernedly. "He is returning to consciousness, alas."

Osbern opened his eyes and at once saw the tall figure of his chieftain. He stared at Woden as if he feared he was gazing at an apparition.

"You asked to see me, I understand," Woden said curtly.

"Cerdic said you would not come, my lord. He said you would have no truck with. . . ." Osbern paused confusedly and seemed to be losing consciousness again.

"I am here, Osbern," Woden said enigmatically.

"My lord, I wish to die," Osbern said then in a firm voice.

"Why do you so wish?"

"The pain is great, my lord."

"The pain will lessen in time."

"If I recover, I shall be a helpless cripple for the rest of my days."

"Why did you do it, Osbern?" Woden asked, evenly.

Osbern said nothing, and turned away from Woden's penetrating gaze.

"Why did you act the traitor, Osbern?" Woden persisted.

Osbern looked at Woden. "You are asking why I stepped from the battle circle and tried to turn the warriors against you? I cannot say, my lord. It was as if a giant hand flung me forward, or perchance one of my comrades. . . ." He paused uncertainly.

"He is delirious, my lord," Ricole interposed. "He knows not what he says. He does not mean to cast suspicion on others."

"You misunderstand me, Osbern," Woden said steadily. "I am already aware of why you stepped from the battle circle, and why you disobeyed my orders. When I ask why you acted the traitor, I refer to your visit to the Saxon burgh and your conversation with Earl Seaxwulf."

Osbern gazed at Woden in horrified silence. How has he learned of my visit to the Haeward burgh? he asked himself. My actions today did not make that plain. Has one of the wounded Saxons spoken of it? Nay, I think not, for they are all warriors of low status and would not have been in Earl Seaxwulf's confidence. Have my henchmen given me away? Nay, for in so doing they would have revealed that they too were party to my plan. Loki take him, I believe Earl Woden has powers of divination!

"Since you fear to answer my question and the matter clearly troubles your conscience, I will give you the answer. I will tell you why you paid a visit to Earl Seaxwulf. You intended, by selling out your people to the Saxons, to become their chieftain, but a chieftain subordinate to Seaxwulf."

"Nay, you are wrong. . . ."

Woden ignored the interruption. "That was what was agreed betwixt Seaxwulf and yourself. But you were not even prepared to be loyal to your new ally, were you, Osbern? You intended using him to achieve the chieftainship and the lady Ricole. . . ."

Woden heard Ricole's indrawn gasp of astonishment and dismay.

"You are talking to a very sick man, my lord," she remonstrated.

But Ricole's interruption, like Osbern's, went unheeded.

". . . and you intended later to throw off the Saxon yoke also," Woden continued.

"How do you know these things, my lord?" asked Osbern hoarsely.

"Was it not as I say, Osbern?" Woden demanded. "Were you not prepared in truth to play the double traitor? Did you not speak with a forked tongue, in both swearing allegiance to me and allying yourself with Seaxwulf?"

"*Ja*, my lord," Osbern admitted wearily.

"Thanks be to the gods, your plan misfired. The Angles were not in such a state of chaos as you and your false ally envisaged, for as you now know to your cost the Saxons have no more liking for a traitor than have the Angles," Woden said. "Unbeknown to you, even your hired henchmen vowed allegiance to me."

"So it was my henchmen who gave me away," Osbern said angrily.

"Nay, curiously, they remained true to me throughout the battle but they did not give you away."

"How then did you discover the truth?" asked Osbern suspiciously.

"How is of no importance," Woden said coldly. "That I did discover it and was prepared for your action today, is of paramount importance."

"My lord, I admit I acted shamefully and that my actions were unforgivable. Henceforth I shall be an outcast from my people," Osbern said, biting his lip against a groan of agony. "I wish only for death."

"Twenty Anglian warriors died today, Osbern, thanks in part to your scheming."

"I know that, my lord, and the knowledge is unbearable," Osbern said bitterly. "That is why I asked to see you. As my lord, it is your duty to administer justice, is it not? That being so, I beg that you pierce my heart with your sword. I do not wish to live, and deserve to die."

"I have no sword," Woden told him, "and am at present unarmed."

Osbern stared at Woden's waist-belt as if to verify this astonishing fact. So my lord Woden has not come here to kill me as I imagined, he thought in surprise.

"Then, my lord, I beseech you throttle me with your own hands," he pleaded. "'Twould be an act of mercy. As an outcast and a helpless cripple, I could not survive for long anyway, and would die slowly and painfully. Kill me, my lord. You, who I have wronged so greatly, alone have the right. Too late I realise your worth."

"What if the gods were to give you another chance?" asked Woden. "Would you use it to commit further acts of treachery?"

"What use such a question, my lord?" Osbern asked, hopelessly. "You torment me in speaking thus. Too late I recognise your worth, that under your leadership the Angles could in time become a great people—not just one small tribe, but a people of many tribes like the Saxons and the Jutes."

"You mean that, Osbern?" Woden asked, gravely.

"As a doomed man, what would I gain by speaking aught but the truth, my lord?"

"You will not die for a long while yet, Osbern," Woden said surprisingly. "The gods are not ready for you."

"Then you refuse to end my miserable existence, my lord?" groaned Osbern. "You will not spare me the torment of a warrior forced to exist without legs?"

"Listen to me, Osbern, listen to me carefully," Woden said, his voice suddenly compassionate. "When I hung for nine nights on the tree, I too suffered pain, I too prayed for death. But the gods had not forsaken me. They taught me how to endure pain and they taught me many other things also, in order that eventually good might come out of evil. They taught me nine songs, and I mastered charms twice times nine."

As he spoke, Woden drew back the blankets which covered Osbern and began to untie the bandages that swathed his injured legs. Then he removed the tourniquet. The tourniquet was a means of stopping the bleeding and of thus saving Osbern's life, but by stopping the blood circulating, it would in time cause the limbs to turn gangrenous and make amputation a necessity.

The blood immediately started to flow from the wounds, spurting in a small fountain from a severed artery and causing Osbern to cry out in pain and fear.

"So this is how you mean to kill me, my lord," Osbern moaned. "I know I deserve such treatment but I beg you have mercy—take the lady Ricole's knife and plunge it deep into my breast."

"Be at peace, Osbern," Woden said reassuringly. "My lady wife will leave us for a few minutes, and you will close your eyes and pray to the gods for forgiveness and the chance to atone for your crime against your people."

Woden turned to Ricole. "I pray you go, my lady, and prepare two poultices large enough to encase Osbern's legs. Prepare them from nine herbs as follows: thyme, fennel, hemlock, deadly nightshade, laurel leaves, nettle, hawthorn, hazel shoots, and myrrh. When they are ready, bring them to me here."

Mystified but trusting her husband implicitly, Ricole went away to prepare the poultices.

Woden turned all his attention on Osbern.

"Close your eyes, as I said," he ordered sternly.

Strangely affected by Woden's compelling gaze, Osbern obeyed.

"Now," Woden said calmly, placing his right hand on

Osbern's forehead, "offer up your mind and your prayers to the gods, and leave your body and wounds to me. Concentrate hard—nay, harder than that—forget me and all earthly matters, rid your mind of fear and guilt and dwell for a short space of time with the gods, and I shall rid you of the pain. . . ."

Woden next placed his hands on Osbern's shattered and still-bleeding legs. He pressed down quite firmly, a hand on each leg, but Osbern made no movement or response, as if he no longer felt pain and were unaware of Woden's touch.

Woden's voice was calm and practical.

"As for bone wrench, as for bone wrench, as for bone wrench," he said, placing cool finger-tips first on Osbern's ankles, then on his knees, and then on his thighs.

"As for blood-wrench, as for blood-wrench, as for blood-wrench," he said, again placing his finger-tips on Osbern's ankles, knees and thighs.

"As for limb-wrench, as for limb-wrench, as for limb-wrench," he said, once more placing his finger-tips on Osbern's ankles, knees and thighs.

Woden moved to the foot of the mattress and grasped Osbern's ankles in strong hands.

"Bone to bone, sinew to sinew, blood to blood, limb to limb, flesh to flesh: heal in the name of Allfather, of the goddess Freya, and of all the company of heaven," he said, jerking each leg quite sharply before replacing it upon the bed.

Osbern still made no sound, as if he were quite oblivious of the drastic treatment being meted out to his shattered limbs.

Woden turned to see Ricole standing beside him, holding the herbal poultices. He took them from her and laid them carefully around Osbern's legs.

"Bandage his legs tightly, little one," he said to Ricole

then. "Thyme, fennel, hemlock, deadly nightshade, laurel leaves, nettle, hawthorn, hazel shoots, and myrrh, are nine herbs great in power. Allfather, the oldest and wisest of the gods, placed them in the Seven Worlds to aid all, rich and poor, and the sky gods taught me their worth whilst I hung on the tree."

"Osbern looks very peaceful, my lord," Ricole said, moving closer to look at the invalid. "Has he fainted from the pain or have you given him another infusion of poppy juice?"

"Neither, little one," Woden answered with a smile, touched by her compassion for the injured man. "He has fallen into a natural slumber. He will sleep till morning and by then he will have little more than scarring and bruising of which to boast."

* * *

"My lord, what of Osbern?" asked Cerdic of Woden ten days later.

"What of him?" asked Woden in surprise. "What troubles you—has he not fully recovered the use of his legs?"

"His recovery is miraculous, my lord," Cerdic acknowledged. "'Tis little more than a week since he was injured but already he displays only a slight limp. Perchance his injuries were less serious than was at first thought."

"You could say that, Cerdic," Woden said non-committally. "But if it is not Osbern's health that concerns you, what in the name of the gods does?"

"His future, my lord," Cerdic said steadily. "He is a traitor and, as such, deserves death."

"He has learned his lesson," Woden said evenly.

"By Frigg!" exclaimed Cerdic explosively. "You are

surely not suggesting he should go unpunished!"

"His own conscience is punishment enough," Woden said imperturbably.

"Then he is not to be banished from Angel as is expected, my lord?"

"Only if the *fyrd*, as tribal justice court, decides it so."

"The *fyrd*, my lord, will be governed by your wishes in the matter," Cerdic pointed out with some truth. "And Osbern, a man who showed himself to be your enemy and the enemy of his people, will escape justice."

"Were not you once my enemy, Cerdic?" asked Woden dispassionately.

"To my shame, *ja*."

"And you are now my friend, are you not? In your heart, I mean, for only the gods and yourself know what you feel in your heart."

"In my heart, my very dear lord, I shall be loyal and true to you till the day I die," Cerdic said resolutely. "It is my earnest desire that when the gods take you, they will take me also—am I not the leader of your *hearth-horde*, the defender of your left arm?"

"Osbern also was once my enemy," Woden said coolly.

"Once!" exclaimed Cerdic scornfully.

"He also is now my friend. In his heart, I mean, for only the gods and Osbern himself know what he feels in his heart," Woden said, smiling wickedly as he repeated his own words—and Cerdic's reply! "In his heart, my very dear Cerdic, he will be loyal and true to me till the day he dies."

"You mock me!" said Cerdic aggrievedly. "You mock me with my own words! Osbern is not as I, my lord."

"Nay, he is not as you, Cerdic. There is a difference," Woden said, his eyes twinkling. "When the gods take me, you say, you desire that they will take you also, as the defender of my left arm. Osbern is different. Osbern desires that when the gods take me, they will take him also, as the defender of my right arm."

"Blood of the gods! You mean. . . ." Further words failed Cerdic and he lapsed into a disapproving silence.

"*Ja*, Osbern is to become deputy leader of my *hearth-horde*," Woden said coolly.

"With respect, my lord, is such a decision wise?" asked Cerdic stiffly. "Osbern is a self-confessed traitor, a man abhorred by our people."

"I shall lead the way in unconditionally forgiving Osbern his transgressions against myself—others will follow my example," Woden said determinedly.

"Never could I forgive such villainy, my lord," Cerdic said emphatically. "And 'tis certain our people will feel as I."

"You could, Cerdic, and you will," Woden said sternly. "I shall make plain my forgiveness of Osbern by making him deputy leader of my *hearth-horde*. He has a strong claim to the chieftainship and saw me, a chieftain who is not an Angle, as a usurper—let us not forget those facts, my friend. I shall show clemency, you will do likewise, and nine days from now Osbern will have become once more an accepted and valuable member of the tribe. Humans, when allowed to forget, have short memories: Osbern will be no more than a nine days' wonder."

"Nine days, you say, my lord?" asked Cerdic.

"*Ja*, nine days."

Cerdic chuckled suddenly, light-heartedly.

"When you quote the figure nine at me, my lord," he said, "I know there is no gainsaying you."

SEVENTEEN

On a certain day in the winter of the following year, Woden was with his warriors in the Heorot when two midwives, their faces beaming amidst the sudden silence, the hush of expectancy that had followed their arrival, gave him the news.

"My lord, all is well," said one. "Your lady wife has given birth to a healthy son."

There was a deafening burst of cheering from the warriors at this announcement.

"He is a beautiful child, my lord," added the other midwife, determined not to be outdone.

"And my lady wife?" asked Woden. "She is well?"

"Never better, my lord, praise be to Freya," beamed the first midwife. "The birth was easy and without complications. Your lady wife is naturally weary and needs rest after her labours, but she awaits you in her bower. . . ."

The midwife's sentence tailed off into silence and she shrugged and exchanged amused glances with her companion, for Woden was already striding swiftly down the Heorot towards the entrance, to the accompaniment of noisy cheers from the warriors, the enthusiastic raising aloft of drinking horns, and to toasts of "The atheling! The atheling!"

Woden rapidly made his way to his dwelling where already a servant was holding wide the entrance door. He briefly acknowledged the servant's smiling congratulations and strode along the passageway to the bower. He opened the door, stepped inside, and closed the door quietly behind him.

He stood for a moment in silence, gazing across the intervening space at his wife and son, savouring the moment.

Understanding his feelings and his silence, Ricole watched him lovingly, her own face shining with happiness. She watched the smile which overspread his features reach his eyes, giving a rare warmth to the cold beauty of his face

She held the infant, cocooned in a woollen blanket, out to him.

"Your son, my lord," she said.

Woden took the infant and kissed him gently on the forehead.

" 'Tis said that no child brings as much joy as a first-born," he said, gazing down at the tiny face, at the delicate fair skin, the wisps of blond hair and the minute fingers that peeped out from the blanket. "He is very beautiful."

"So they told you!" Ricole said, mischievously. "The midwives told you he is a tiny replica of yourself—yet still you admire his beauty!"

"Nay, they said nothing of a likeness, did they, my atheling?" Woden said softly, addressing the infant. "And beautiful you are, for you have your mama's beautiful blue eyes, have you not?"

"All new-born infants have blue eyes," Ricole told him. "In a few weeks' time perchance they will change to green like yours. What shall we call him, my lord?"

"Wihtlaeg," Woden answered quietly, as if already he had considered the matter. "If you have no objection, my lady."

Ricole took the baby from him then and cradled him tenderly against her breast. "Nay, we have no objection, have we, little Wihtlaeg? You are the atheling, born to be a leader of men, and Wihtlaeg is a strong name, a fine name, for such a one."

"And what of you, beloved?" Woden asked, anxiously. "You need rest they tell me, so. . . ."

"Oh, my lord, I am so happy, so ecstatically happy, at this moment," Ricole interposed. "If only we could remain thus for ever—just you, me and our baby."

"I think little Wihtlaeg would not thank you for wishing eternal babyhood on him," smiled Woden.

"You are right of course, my lord," Ricole sighed. "And yet he is so enchanting as he is. One day he will be a grown man, a warrior, he will kill and face death and. . . ."

"Stop! Stop!" exclaimed Woden with mock severity. "The little fellow has only just been born and already his mama has him almost dead and buried."

"Oh, my lord, whatever should I do without you!" Ricole exclaimed, laughing at her own foolishness.

"You may one day learn the answer to that question," Woden said practically.

"Do not speak thus!" Ricole exclaimed, tears starting to her eyes. "Should you die, my lord, then must I die also!"

" 'Twas you, not I, who spoke of dying, beloved," Woden reminded her. "I was not referring to my death."

"Then to what were you referring, my lord?"

"One day, my lady, I must return to my homeland," Woden answered evenly.

"Oh, that!" said Ricole lightly, brushing aside her tears. "Of course I understand your desire to visit your homeland. I know how I would feel if I left Angel to dwell in a far-off land. Do not look so sad, my lord, we will not be separated for long—perchance you might even take me with you to meet your people."

"Did I look sad?" asked Woden with a smile. "That was foolish of me on such a day as this, for it is surely the second happiest day of my life."

"The second?" asked Ricole innocently. "What was the first, my lord?"

"The day you became mine, beloved," Woden answered tenderly. "But I do not need to tell you that. I could see from your expression that you already knew it."

"So your first happiness was the cause of your second happiness," said Ricole, her cheeks dimpling.

"Of all my happiness," corrected Woden quietly.

EIGHTEEN

"My lord, I have just returned from Angel."

"Tell me of your visit, Eric," ordered Earl Seaxwulf.

"I found employment as a farm-hand on one of the home-steads as we'd planned, my lord," explained the Saxon. "My presence there for four weeks in such a humble capacity seemingly aroused no suspicions and, by keeping my eyes and ears open, I learned of much that went on in the burgh. Earl Woden is highly esteemed by his people. No chieftain in living memory has won such acclaim as a warrior."

"No chieftain?" frowned Seaxwulf.

"No *Anglian* chieftain, my lord," Eric explained hastily. "One cannot compare a mere Anglian chieftain with a chieftain of your stature."

"The Angles remain loyal to the stranger?" asked Seax-wulf, as if hoping the answer would be in the negative.

"To a man, my lord."

"What of Osbern the traitor?" asked Seaxwulf. "Is he now a lord's man also?"

"There's none more loyal, my lord."

"You surprise me, Eric—when Osbern came to me with his treacherous plan, he seemed a man with a deeply rooted grievance."

"It seems Earl Woden forgave Osbern his treachery and installed him deputy leader of his *hearth-horde*."

"Then Earl Woden is a bigger fool than I thought!" ex-claimed Seaxwulf scornfully. "Once a traitor, always a traitor—the only traitor one can trust, is a dead traitor!"

"That's what I believed, my lord, and doubtless you are right, but. . . ." Eric hesitated, chary of disagreeing with his master.

"But what, Eric? Speak out, man, for Frigg's sake!" Seaxwulf insisted, impatiently.

"From all accounts, Earl Woden is Osbern's hero, the man for whom he'd cheerfully forfeit everything he has, even his life," Eric explained. "Didn't Earl Woden give him back that which was more precious than life itself—his health and his chance to serve? 'Tis said that after our men had shattered Osbern's legs, 'twas thought he'd never walk again, but Earl Woden mended Osbern's legs by a miracle. They also say that the gods taught Earl Woden much wisdom whilst he hung upon the tree."

"He has certainly discovered the trick of bringing good out of evil," Seaxwulf admitted. "Doubtless he has dealings in witchcraft and has bewitched Osbern. Certainly Earl Woden possesses strange powers and his people have been taken in by them. During the two years since Earl Woden's arrival at Angel, I have sent several invasion forces there as you know, but all have been beaten off despite our vastly superior numbers and our highly trained warriors."

"There's only one way to overcome Angel, my lord," said Eric.

Seaxwulf nodded. "*Ja*, to first overcome and destroy Earl Woden. But that is easier said than done. Or has your espial of Angel given you an idea? Have you found an Angle who can be corrupted into our service?"

"Nay, my lord, there's no possibility of that," Eric answered emphatically. "So dearly is Earl Woden loved and so ably is he protected, that there's not even the possibility of ambushing him when he goes hunting. Whilst he himself is curiously careless of his safety, his faithful Cerdic and Osbern more than compensate for his carelessness. They see to it that he never rides out without a strong escort, and the sizeable force we should need to overcome such an escort, could scarcely remain undetected in the forest. There's only one occasion when, at his own insistence, Earl Woden is without his faithful warriors."

"Tell me of it," ordered Seaxwulf.

"On the tenth day of *Thrimilci*, the anniversary month of his arrival at Angel, Earl Woden and his lady spend the night in a cave on the edge of the forest, near the temple of Freya. The place holds some special meaning for him, his people believe, although Earl Woden himself never speaks of it. Last year, on the first anniversary of his arrival, he and the lady Ricole spent the night there, and nine months later, on the anniversary of the birth of the atheling Wihtlaeg, the lady Ricole gave birth to twin sons Baeldaeg and Waegdaeg. Four weeks from now 'twill again be the anniversary of Earl Woden's arrival, and his people clearly expect that he'll again retreat to the cave with his lady."

"You are suggesting that we ambush him there?" asked Seaxwulf interestedly.

"No better opportunity will present itself, my lord, I'm convinced of that," Eric answered. "The cave is about a quarter of a mile from the burgh and Earl Woden insists on going there without his *hearth-horde*. He strolls off into the forest, his people say joyfully, like a lover with his lass."

"As you say, Eric, we shall get no better opportunity," Seaxwulf agreed enthusiastically. "Half a dozen warriors would be enough to carry out our purpose and, disguised as huntsmen, they could easily infiltrate the forest around Angel without arousing suspicion. Earl Woden must be ambushed and killed. As one of my most experienced warriors, Eric, and one well acquainted with the area around Angel, you shall lead the ambush."

"Thank you, my lord," Eric said. "I shall not fail you. What of the lady Ricole?"

"She must be taken prisoner," Seaxwulf said decisively. "As the daughter of that doughty old warrior, Earl Leofgar, she is dearly loved by the Angles and will be held hostage for the future submission of her people."

"*Ja*, my lord, it shall be as you say."

Seaxwulf chuckled wickedly. "I might even take the lady Ricole to wife, Eric. She is a comely lass by all accounts and breeds easily it seems. Since the recent death of my wife in childbed, having only a daughter to show for twenty years of marriage, a new bride is just what I need. See she comes to no harm, Eric. Go to it—kill Earl Woden and win your lord a new lady and you shall be well rewarded."

*   *   *

"How good it is to be here with you again, my lord," Ricole sighed rapturously as she lay beside Woden in the cave on the tenth night of *Thrimilci*. " 'Tis two years since our first meeting and already we have three sons. Sometimes our first meeting seems as yesterday, and at other times I cannot recall life without you."

The cave had been swept clean by servants in readiness for their annual visit, and sweet-smelling herbs had been sprinkled on the rocky floor. The oil lamp was there as before but now a low bed, furnished with fur skins had been placed there, and another fur skin was draped across the entrance, keeping out the chill night air.

"Time is relative, beloved," Woden answered obscurely.

"Why do we come here, my lord?"

"I am surprised that you ask such a question, my lady,"

Woden said sternly. "I had hoped it was obvious why we came here. Does it not give us an opportunity to be alone, really alone, an opportunity to relive our first mating?"

"But we are really alone when we lie in our bower, my lord, are we not? Or have Cerdic and Osbern been with us and I have not noticed?" Ricole asked, flippantly.

"Sometimes I think they would like to be!"

"My lord, you shock me!" Ricole said demurely. pretending to misunderstand. "I assure you I have no desire to bed with Cerdic or Osbern."

"I am glad to hear it," said Woden with mock severity, but then he chuckled. "In fact Osbern did suggest he should accompany us here tonight."

"Mother of the gods!"

"He would remain outside the entrance, he told me magnanimously, but he feared that if ever our enemies should learn of our coming here alone, an attempt might be made on my life."

"Osbern could well be right, my lord," Ricole said in sudden anxiety. "Perchance you should have hearkened to him and agreed, rather than have come here without a guard."

"I am not without protection," Woden told her lightly. "I have my spear, and Huginn perches only a few feet from the entrance."

"Huginn? *Ja*, I saw him when we arrived—and he has company!" Ricole said, with a smile.

"Muninn, you mean?"

"Muninn? Is that her name?"

"That is my name for her. Huginn calls her 'Caw-caw' most of the time. Like his lord, Huginn has found a mate, and has built a nest for them at the top of the Sacred Tree. I think Huginn, too, expects to become a father in a few weeks' time."

"How do you know that?" asked Ricole, not sure if he were serious.

"A little bird told me."

"I believe coming here like this means more to you than you will admit, my lord," Ricole said thoughtfully.

"There are times, my lady, when I suspect that you can read my mind," Woden chuckled. "You are right. There is another reason for my wishing to come here alone."

"Tell me, my lord," Ricole said, leaning over to kiss him lovingly.

"Sometimes I need to be alone in order to remember that I am not an Angle and that I have another home. Sometimes I need to separate myself from the Angles and all they mean to me, to regain my perspective of the past and of the future."

"Alone, you say?" Ricole pouted. "Would you rather I were not here?"

"You and I are one, beloved," Woden said, kissing her, "in the stream of divine life."

"You speak strangely, my lord."

"I have neither the need nor desire to separate myself from you," Woden assured her.

"You spoke just now of the future, my lord—what meant you?"

"Cast your mind back to the night of our first meeting here, little one. I spoke then of my mission here at Angel and told you that when it was accomplished, I should take you away to the land of my people."

Ricole nodded. "*Ja*, I recall you telling me that much must remain unexplained until that time came, and you asked me to trust you. I have always trusted you, my lord. I recall too when Wihtlaeg was born, how you spoke then of visiting your homeland."

"I said I must one day return to my homeland," Woden

said with careful emphasis.

Ricole looked at him for a moment in silence, her mind arrested by his sober expression.

"*Ja*, my lord—" she said slowly, as if testing his reaction, "—on a visit."

Woden made no response.

"Only for a visit," Ricole persisted, trying to keep the tremor of fear from her voice. "You will come back to Angel of course."

Woden put an arm around her and drew her close.

"Nay, little one," he said gravely, "when I return to my homeland, there I shall remain."

"You surely cannot mean that, my lord," Ricole protested tearfully.

"I mean it."

"You will leave Angel for good?"

"*Ja*."

"You will leave your people to their own devices?"

"They are not my people, sweeting—they are my adopted people. My people dwell a great distance from Angel."

"You will leave Angel. . . ." Ricole paused, as if steeling herself to utter the heart-rending words. "And me?"

"I did not say that," Woden reminded her. "On the contrary, I spoke of taking you with me."

"But is that not what you meant, my lord?" Ricole wept. "Did not you in truth mean to leave me also?"

Woden's arm tightened consolingly around her. "Listen, Ricole. Listen carefully. One day in the future, many years hence, I must return to my homeland. I have no choice. You, little one, have a choice. You can come with me or you can remain here at Angel with your people."

"Then the choice is simple," Ricole said, a happy smile banishing her tears. "Of course I shall come with you. Would I choose to remain here with my people, instead of accompanying my lord?"

"By 'your people', I meant also your children, our children," Woden explained.

Ricole's smile faded. "You mean we would leave our children here, our little Wihtlaeg and the twins?" she demanded.

"We could not take them with us. Their place is here, for their future is here," Woden said resolutely. "They are part of my mission here."

"Why do you tell me this now, on the second anniversary of our first loving?" Ricole asked, reproachfully. "I was so happy."

"I am telling you because I want you to know the truth, little one," Woden said patiently. "I want you to know what the future holds for us, and I want you to be prepared. One day you will have to make a difficult decision."

"But I fail to understand, my lord—why could our children not accompany us to your homeland?"

"As I told you, their future is here. They will be the founders of a new dynasty. They will be rulers," Woden explained. "The tribe will grow and spread its wings, and our children and our grandchildren will become the leaders of a great people. That is their destiny. My destiny lies with my own people."

"Whither lies my destiny?" Ricole asked, a trifle coldly.

"Only you can answer that question, beloved," Woden said sadly. "You are the wife of a stranger. . . ."

"The Angles no longer regard you as a stranger, as well you know, my lord," Ricole interposed.

"The Angles, like you, beloved, have accepted me on trust," Woden said quietly. "What do they know of me? Do they know whence I came? Do they know who sired me? Do they know how I journeyed here? Nay, in truth I am still a stranger, a man who must one day return whence he came. You are the wife of a stranger, and the mother of future leaders of your people. Only you can decide whither lies your destiny."

"Holy Freya, what am I to do!" Ricole exclaimed, unhappily.

Leaning over, Woden kissed her and then, a trifle sardonically, gazed down at her.

"One day, a long time hence, with the sky gods' help, you will make your decision and it will be the right decision," he said tenderly. "But not now, my lady. Now, there are better things for us to do."

"Like begetting another little orphan?" asked Ricole bitterly.

"Like begetting another little infant who will have become a big strong warrior before his mother need make her decision," Woden said firmly. "Curious, is it not? Usually it is the younglings who fly the nest—in this case it could well be the oldsters! I wonder what decision Muninn will make."

The soft silky sensuousness of the fur skin on which she lay, was warm and comforting to Ricole's naked body, and aided Woden's caresses in banishing her troubled thoughts to the back of her mind. She sighed ecstatically. One day I must make a decision, an agonising decision, she said to herself, but not for a long while yet. Much can change with the passing of time. One cannot look far into the future. Perchance my lord will change his mind, will become so bound up with the Angles that he will be unable to bring himself to leave. The future must wait. 'Tis the present that matters, and at present I am blissfully happy in the arms of my lord. All the same. . . .

"You are pensive, little one," Woden said softly.

"I was. I am not any more," Ricole said passionately.

With one swift movement, she clasped his head in her

hands, drew it down to her breast and offered him one of her nipples.

His mouth closed on her breast and he sucked gently, so that she sighed and moaned in an ecstasy of pleasure and excitement.

"You have never done that before," he murmured, as he released her nipple.

"I have not been called upon to make an agonising decision before," she answered breathlessly. "I have just made my decision. You are all in all to me. You are my lord, my husband, my lover, and the child at my breast. I could not separate myself from you, even for our children's sake."

He took her then, in a sudden access of joy and delight.

Held fast in his embrace, feeling the thrust of his body in hers, murmuring incoherent words of pleasure and endearment, Ricole's mind was nonetheless detached from their love-making in a way she could not have explained.

Woden is mine, she thought. On this one night of the year, I share him with no other, not even with my children. On this one night of the year, before his seed enters my belly and gives life to another child, we are alone and together. Is such possible? Is it not a contradiction in terms. Nay, in being alone and together, we are one.

We are one. To separate myself from Woden would be like cutting out my own heart. Either way I should die. We are one. . . .

NINETEEN

Ricole awoke at the first light of dawn and lay, warm and relaxed, thinking about the joys of the past night. The interior of the cave was dim and shadowy, only a single shaft of light bypassing the curtained entrance.

She turned to look at Woden and was surprised to see that he was wide awake. He put his fingers to his lips as if bidding her to remain silent and then clasped one of her hands in his under the fur coverlet.

Ricole gazed at him in astonishment. Why is he acting so strangely? she thought. Why must I remain silent? As Woden's hand touched hers, Ricole heard a voice, Woden's voice, answering her thoughts and communicating his urgent message to her. Neither his lips nor a muscle of his face moved: it was as if the words leapt into Ricole's mind instead of into her ears.

"Trust me and do exactly as I, the lord of the raven, tell you, Ricole," the voice said. "Nay, do not speak or show surprise. Lie calm and relaxed as if nothing were toward. There are Saxons lurking outside the entrance. If I move, they will spring at me. When I release your hand, that is your signal. The Saxons will not be disquieted when you move, for it is part of their plan to separate us. At the signal, arise unconcernedly from the bed and go to the back of the cave, as if to quench your thirst from the water-jug. Drink some water and remain there until I tell you to take hold of my spear, Gungnir, which stands close to the water-jug. Then do exactly as I say without question or hesitation. Do not be afraid. All will be well if you follow my instructions. Go, now!"

As Woden released her hand, despite the thumping of her heart, Ricole managed to make a convincing display of arising sleepily and carelessly from the bed. She stretched herself lethargically, drew on her fur-trimmed mantle, and then stepped lightly to the back of the cave. She poured some water into a drinking mug and took a few sips of the water, registering as she did so the exact position of Woden's spear. It was now within her hand's reach.

There was a sudden disturbance at the cave's entrance, the sound of rushing feet and, looking round in alarm, Ricole saw six Saxon warriors, their seaxes drawn, push swiftly past the entrance curtain and make towards Woden.

With a cry of "Gungnir!" Woden sprang to his feet.

As Ricole obediently seized the spear, Woden leapt nimbly aside just as the first man, his seax raised to strike and misjudging Woden's speed, rushed at him, missed him and went headlong past him into the rocky wall, to fall back stunned upon the floor.

Facing the other five Saxons, his great height giving him an advantage, Woden kicked out viciously at one of them, causing the man to lose his grip on his seax, whilst at the same time Woden called out to Ricole.

"When I call the name 'Gungnir!', point the spear at the man I indicate," he ordered.

"I know not how to use a spear!" Ricole cried, in dismay.

"Just point it at the man I indicate, that is all," Woden answered firmly.

As the second warrior grovelled for his fallen seax, Woden kicked it away from him across the cave and turned to face the four armed men. One, seeing Woden's attention momentarily engaged, crept up behind him to deliver a treacherous blow from the rear but, sensing his danger, Woden turned swiftly, leapt to one side and issued his command to Ricole.

"Gungnir!" he cried.

Ricole pointed the spear at the Saxon and nearly collapsed with shock and surprise at what happened next. The man was suddenly illuminated by a brilliant white light, a light so bright that it temporarily dimmed Ricole's sight, and then he disintegrated into a pile of ashes.

Two of the remaining three armed warriors gazed in stupefaction at the remains of their comrade, but the third, more quick-witted than his fellows, saw his opportunity and, with a furious oath, sprang at Woden.

Kicking out at his adversary, Woden struck his legs from under him and then leapt backward, again calling to Ricole.

"Gungnir!" he cried.

Ricole pointed the spear at the Saxon who, from a kneeling position, lunged out fiercely at Woden with his seax, narrowly missing him. But then he, too, was illuminated by a brilliant light and was instantaneously reduced to a pile of ashes.

This last happening had taken only a few seconds but it had given the remaining two armed men time to recover their wits. Enraged by the treatment meted out to their comrades, they turned a concerted attack on Woden. One had retrieved the seax of the second fallen man and, ambidextrous like all his race, now held a seax in each hand. Both men advanced steadily towards Woden, one from his left and the other from his right. Woden, unarmed, backed away until his back came up against the wall of the cave and he was seemingly at their mercy. As, grinning evilly, the Saxons came to within striking distance, Woden leapt into action. Bounding between and beyond them, he turned, banged their heads together with his powerful hands, seized the fur coverlet from the bed and flung it over their heads.

"Gungnir!" he cried to Ricole.

In a matter of seconds both men, their seaxes, and the fur coverlet had dissolved into a pile of ashes.

"Look out, my lord!" Ricole cried, urgently. "The man who dropped his seax has seized that of the first man, and is behind you!"

Woden turned swiftly to see the Saxon advancing stealthily towards him.

"You murdering son of Loki!" cried the enraged man. "I know not what devil's trickery you used to destroy my comrades, but ye'll not get me!"

He leapt at Woden, grazing Woden's arm with his seax and causing him to step swiftly backwards. In so doing, Woden tripped over the stunned man who was now showing signs of regaining consciousness.

This time, Ricole needed no prompting. Her lord was in danger of his life. As Woden fell and the Saxon leapt to the attack, she called a warning to Woden and pointed the spear at the Saxon.

"Gungnir!" she cried.

Woden rolled aside out of range of the lethal weapon, and the irate Saxon met the same fate as his comrades.

The stunned man, having fully recovered his senses, had nevertheless been pinned to the ground by Woden's prostrate body. Previously oblivious of what had been going on around him, he had witnessed the disintegration of his one remaining comrade with open-mouthed horror and disbelief.

"Where is Sceaf?" he gasped foolishly. "He has vanished into thin air!"

Woden stood up and pointed to the small pile of ashes.

"Those, alas, are the remains of your comrade," he said

evenly and, pointing to the other ashes, "and those are the remains of the others. Look well on them, Saxon. You and your comrades thought to ambush the lord Woden when he lacked the protection of his *hearth-horde*, did you not?"

"Spare me, my lord," the Saxon pleaded, remaining on his knees as Woden went to take the spear from Ricole's trembling hands.

"Are you all right, little one?" Woden asked, concerned by Ricole's pallor. "You look a little shaken."

"I am a little shaken, my lord," Ricole admitted ruefully. " 'Tis not every day that one is called upon to cremate five warriors in almost as many seconds. You must be patient with me. I am not a practised spearswoman and still have much to learn!"

Woden smiled at her rueful expression and, placing a strong supporting arm about her waist, turned to the still-kneeling warrior.

"Your name?" he enquired courteously.

"Eric, my lord."

"Go, Eric," Woden said. "Return to Earl Seaxwulf and tell him what has befallen your comrades."

"You are letting me go, my lord?" asked Eric incredulously. "You are not going to kill me?"

"And leave Earl Seaxwulf without the knowledge of his men's fate?" Woden smiled. "Without such knowledge, he might even be tempted to try to ambush me again!"

"You bear me no malice?" asked Eric, seemingly unable to believe his luck.

"Malice?" Woden shook his head. "You are a Saxon, the traditional enemy of the Angles. You did only that which you had to do: you obeyed the commands of your lord. Tell Earl Seaxwulf from me that I send him cordial greetings, I condole with him over the unfortunate loss of his warriors, and I pray that the day is not far distant when he and I shall meet as friends instead of enemies. That day will surely come."

"I shall tell Earl Seaxwulf all you say, my lord," said Eric, getting a little unsteadily to his feet.

"One more thing, Eric," Woden said.

"*Ja*, my lord?"

"Tell Earl Seaxwulf that much as I regret his loss of his lady wife, he must seek elsewhere for a replacement." Woden smiled wickedly. "The lady Ricole is mine."

"How did you know that was part of the plan, my lord?" asked Eric in surprise.

"How did my lord know what was part of the plan?" asked Ricole suspiciously.

The Saxon looked discomfited in the face of Ricole's enquiry, and Woden calmly came to his rescue.

"How did I know of Earl Seaxwulf's plans for my lady's future, you ask?" he said evenly. "Know your enemy, Saxon. That is the first precept of knowledge. I know my enemy. Earl Seaxwulf did not."

"I will give Earl Seaxwulf your messages, my lord, and will be on my way," Eric said.

"Earl Seaxwulf has no atheling, I understand," Woden said, with seeming inconsequence.

"That is so, my lord."

"He has a daughter, has he not, Eric?"

"He has, my lord—the lady Seaxburh is a dainty little maid who is nearing her second summer."

"Tell Earl Seaxwulf that my atheling is of a similar age to his daughter," Woden said. "He will understand my meaning."

PART II

THE DEPARTURE

TWENTY

Five thousand four hundred and eighty-seven years had now passed since the beginning of the world, and eighteen years—twice times nine—since Woden's arrival at Angel. During those eighteen years, Ricole had borne Woden nine children, the atheling Wihtlaeg, the twins Baeldaeg and Waegdaeg, Wyrt, Sigehelm, Cuthred, Wecta, Edwin, and the only girl child Nigon.[1]

Under Woden's brilliant leadership, the Angles had become renowned as fighting men: as formidable and respected foes and as loyal and courageous allies. The tribe had prospered in all ways. With Woden's approval, some of the younger noblemen had spread their wings and gone to live in other places, where they had founded new tribes and built new burghs, whilst still maintaining allegiance to Woden as their overlord and as the arbiter of territorial disputes within all the Anglian domains. Three years after his arrival, Woden had led the first Anglian expedition to the shores of Roman-occupied Britain. The Angles had crossed the uncharted seas in their shallow, mastless boats and had raided Roman cities and encampments, destroying all who opposed them and plundering cattle, slaves, and treasure-chests of silver and gold. They had remained in Britain for many days, exploring and reconnoitring that green and pleasant land.

In eighteen years, Woden had accomplished his purpose.

[1] Old English word meaning "nine".

His atheling Wihtlaeg who, as with all Woden's sons, bore a close resemblance to him, had been trained for leadership and was already courageous and wise beyond his years. Wihtlaeg would soon be ready to take his father's place.

On the evening of the eighteenth anniversary of Woden's arrival, he returned to his dwelling at an unusually early hour. Except at festival times and other special occasions, it was customary for him and his warriors to sup in the Heorot, whilst the womenfolk remained in their own dwellings or apartments. When supper was over, Woden usually remained for some time in the Heorot, discussing tribal matters and conversing and jesting with his men. But that evening, wishing to speak to Ricole alone, he left the Heorot early and went to his dwelling where he found her alone in their living-chamber as he had expected.

" 'Tis good to have your company so early in the evening, my lord," Ricole said, her face lighting up as it always did when she saw him.

"With Nigon abed and our sons occupied with their own affairs, I guessed I would find you alone at this hour," Woden told her. "There is a matter of some importance I wish to discuss with you, my lady, and I have told the servants we are not to be disturbed."

Woden seated himself on the cushioned, intricately carved bench seat in front of the fire and drew Ricole down beside him.

"Nine months from now, little one, Wihtlaeg will be nearing his eighteenth nativity," he said.

Ricole smiled. "Wihtlaeg's nativity will mark eighteen years, nine months and nine days since first I saw you, my lord," she said happily.

Woden nodded. "Twice times nine, nine months and nine days," he said absently, as if to himself.

"There is sadness in your voice, my lord—why so?"

"When the day of Wihtlaeg's nativity dawns, my task here at Angel will be done," Woden explained dispassionately. "Then must I return to my homeland, to the people from whom I have been so long absent."

Ricole was silent. This is the moment I have dreaded all these years, she thought to herself. This is the moment for which Woden sought to prepare me. But now it has come, I find myself totally unprepared. In my heart, I believed the time would never come when I must make the agonising decision. But have not I already made the decision? Did not I decide long since that I would go with my lord, come what might? All the same, it will be hard, unbelievably hard, to carry through my purpose, to leave my beloved children and my homeland and go to live in an unknown land amongst unknown people. My lord never speaks of his people. When I question him about them, he is evasive and clearly does not wish to speak of them. After all these years, Woden is still in many ways a stranger to me although, in truth, his mystery is in itself a powerful attraction and is one of the reasons why I love him so dearly.

"You speak of your homeland, my lord," she said. "Is Angel not your homeland now? Home is where the heart lies, the travellers say, and is not Angel your homeland in your heart?"

"*Ja*, for much of the time it is," Woden replied almost unwillingly. "When the memory of my true homeland, of my people, and of my family, grows dim, then Angel becomes truly home. But then, prompted perchance by some quite trivial happening, my memory quickens and I recall the beauty of my homeland: nostalgia grips me then and tugs painfully at my heart-strings."

"Beauty?" Ricole asked, a little indignantly. "Is there not beauty here at Angel?"

Woden nodded. "There is beauty, great beauty, for you,

my lady, are here at Angel," he said lovingly.

"But. . . ."

"There is beauty also, beauty greater than you can imagine, in my homeland," Woden continued. "Sleipnir is beautiful."

"Who is Sleipnir?" asked Ricole suspiciously. "Is she your concubine?"

Woden seemed not to have heard the question. "I love Sleipnir dearly," he said effusively.

"You shock me, my lord!" exclaimed Ricole jealously. "So that is why you are so anxious to return."

"That is one of my reasons," Woden admitted coolly. "Sleipnir is mounted frequently."

"Mother of the gods!" exclaimed Ricole angrily. "You mount her frequently you say. Doubtless you yearn for her body, to take her in carnal embrace."

"Carnal embrace?" Woden asked, as if it were his turn to be shocked. "Carnal embrace? Loki's bones! Sleipnir is my stallion."

Ricole flushed, feeling a little foolish. "Much will have changed in the past eighteen years, my lord. Doubtless Sleipnir will have forgotten you."

"Sleipnir will never forget me," Woden said confidently.

"After eighteen years?" she asked scornfully. "He will long since have gone to Valhalla!"

"Sleipnir will be only two years older than when I left my homeland," Woden said.

"How can that be, my lord?" Ricole asked, amusedly. "You are surely jesting."

"My people measure time differently from yours, little one," Woden explained. "Nine of your years are equal to only one of ours."

"But you will be eighteen years older when you return," Ricole pointed out, still not sure if he were serious.

"Do I look eighteen years older?" Woden asked, evenly.

Ricole gazed at him consideringly. "Nay, my lord, you do not. It is curious, but only yesterday Ceolburh remarked upon the fact. ' 'Tis eighteen years since our lord's arrival here, my lady,' she said, 'and yet he looks scarcely any older!' Ceolburh is right. You are little changed from the day I first saw you in the ship on the shore."

"There are many differences between Angel and my homeland, too many to explain to you now, and methinks you could never understand them fully unless you saw them for yourself."

"At least I know you have a stallion and he would not be difficult to understand," Ricole said lightly. "I love horses as you know, my lord, and he and I would soon be the best of friends."

"Sleipnir has eight legs," Woden said coolly.

"Eight legs!" exclaimed Ricole. "Whoever heard of a horse with eight legs? Now I know you are teasing me, my lord."

"Sleipnir has eight legs and two wings."

"A winged horse? You take me back to my childhood, my lord," Ricole smiled. "I can recall sitting round the fire on winter nights listening enthralled to my nurse's tales of winged horses and unicorns. Such stories have been handed down from mother to child through countless generations, but they are no more than childhood tales."

"Or maybe those tales of your childhood had a basis in fact, beloved," Woden pointed out. "Perchance they stem from a time when another man from my homeland came here and told of winged horses and unicorns—*ja*, we have unicorns too! Or perchance there really were winged horses in this land of Denmark many, many centuries ago. Anyway Sleipnir is real enough, I assure you. His eight legs and wings give him great speed. He can gallop over the ground, fly through the sky, and swim in the sea, faster than the speed of. . . ." Woden paused.

"The speed of what, my lord?" asked Ricole.

"Faster than any horse you have seen, little one," Woden said evasively. "Not another word about Sleipnir! Come with me to my homeland and you shall see everything for yourself. My people will love you."

"You know I shall come with you, my lord," Ricole said sadly. "Have not I already told you of my decision? But the thought of leaving our children—especially little Nigon, our last-born—distresses me deeply. Nigon is only in her fourth summer and needs a mother's love."

"With eight doting brothers to love and protect her, and with Ceolburh to nurse her as she already does together with her own children, Nigon will not lack care and affection. And Edwin, the youngest of our sons, is nine years old and already has the makings of a warrior."

"Is Wihtlaeg not over-young for leadership?" Ricole asked, clutching at straws.

"He is ready for leadership," Woden said quietly.

"Have you told him of your decision to return to your homeland, my lord?"

"Nay, not yet. I wished to talk to you first, beloved," Woden answered, "to make sure that you had remained firm in your decision. I shall tell no one till nine days before our departure. I want to give you a chance to change your mind. It is not too late to do so, and I shall not try to influence you if you decide not to come with me."

Her eyes bright with tears, Ricole flung herself into his arms.

"You influence me by just being you, my lord," she said tearfully. "I look at you, I feel your strong arms around me, I hear the joy in your voice when you speak of Sleipnir, I hear the sorrow in your voice when you speak of my not going with you. I shall go with you. I cannot help myself. My life is irresistibly bound up with yours."

Woden held her closely and looked tenderly down at her.

"Trust me, little one, just as you have always trusted me," he said gently. "I know the departure will be hard for you, and that you fear the future in an unknown land, but I promise that you will never regret your decision."

TWENTY-ONE

"Nine days from now, I shall be departing for my home-land, my atheling," Woden said to Wihtlaeg, having summoned him to his private audience chamber. "You will then become the leader of our people."

Wihtlaeg gazed at him enigmatically, as if carefully assimilating the information before making reply.

Wihtlaeg bore a close physical resemblance to his father, having a similar god-like grace, an air of nobility, which set him always a little apart from those around him. Tall and well-made, his shoulder-length blond hair contrasted strikingly with a complexion bronzed by exposure to sea and elements. Like Woden, he possessed an air of remoteness, of mystery: he never showed his feelings, he never spoke without thought or expressed an opinion until he was ready to do so.

"I understand, my lord," he said at length. "When will you return?"

"I shall not return."

Wihtlaeg said nothing and, thinking he had not understood, Woden explained further.

"I shall not return in body, only in spirit," he said. "Part of me will always remain here at Angel, in you and in my other children. My spirit will live on in you."

"I understand, my lord," Wihtlaeg said again.

"You express no surprise, my son?"

"I think in my heart I have always known that you

would one day leave us and return to your homeland, my lord," Wihtlaeg said. "From earliest childhood, I have hearkened to tales of your mysterious arrival at a time of tribal unrest, and the warriors never tire of recounting your deeds and exploits. I accepted the tales and the special knowledge they seemed to bring me, and I also accepted, though I never spoke of it, that you would one day return whence you came. What of my lady mother—have you told her of your departure?"

"She will be going with me, my son," Woden said quietly. "Perchance that surprises you."

Wihtlaeg shook his head. "Recognising the devotion you share with my mother and the happiness each of you feels in the company of the other, nay, it does not surprise me."

"The love I share with your mother defies all description, my son," Woden said quietly.

Wihtlaeg smiled. "One sees it in your eyes as you gaze at my mother, in her eyes as she gazes at you, my lord; in the curve of her lips when she smiles at you, in the silence that sometimes lies between you, a silence that is more expressive than words."

"You speak with the tongue of a poet, my son."

Wihtlaeg shook his head. "Nay, my lord, I am no poet. Wyrt is the poet of the family and expresses his thoughts so much better than I."

"You and your brothers and sister are very close, thanks be to the gods," Woden said.

"Could offspring of such a union as yours, be anything but close, my lord?"

"The knowledge of your devotion each for the other will be a source of great comfort to your mother and me," Woden said earnestly. "After our departure, you, my atheling, will be chieftain of your people and head of the family. Your years are few, my son, but already you show courage and wisdom. You will care for your people and your brothers and sister as does a father for his children."

"In six months' time, my lord, I am to wed the lady Seaxburh," Wihtlaeg reminded him.

Woden nodded. "You have a deep regard for the lady Seaxburh, have you not, my son?"

"Methinks my feelings for the lady Seaxburh have helped me to understand the love you share with my mother," Wihtlaeg confided. "You said a moment ago that I spoke with the tongue of a poet. As I said then, my lord, Wyrt is the poet—I spoke with the tongue of a lover."

Woden smiled. "And it is clear that your regard for the lady Seaxburh is reciprocated, my atheling. As a Saxon, the only child of Earl Seaxwulf, the lady Seaxburh's betrothal to you has at last brought peace with the Saxons, our traditional enemies. 'Tis curious to think that my grandchildren will also be the grandchildren of a Saxon chieftain.

"You will leave here in nine days' time, my lord?" asked Wihtlaeg.

Woden nodded. "In nine days' time, my son, at the ninth hour of the morning."

"That is the time at which you arrived here, from all accounts."

"*Ja*, I arrived at the ninth hour, and shall depart twice times nine years, nine months and nine days later."

"You will leave, as you came, in the ship?" asked Wihtlaeg curiously.

"The ship has remained undisturbed in one of the boathouses since my arrival—it will bear your lady mother and me from these shores on the first part of our journey," Woden told him.

"The first part of your journey, my lord?" asked Wihtlaeg in surprise. "You will not travel all the way in the ship?"

"Nay, my people will be sending another, a faster, vessel for me," Woden said enigmatically. "That is why I must leave at the agreed time."

"It surprises me, my lord, that the ship has remained undisturbed all these years, that no one has ventured to discover its secret, for secrets it has by all accounts," Wihtlaeg said interestedly.

"You have heard of Morcar, my son?"

"*Ja*, my lord."

"Morcar ventured to the boat and took my spear Gungnir —when Morcar died soon afterwards, it was thought by many that he had displeased the sky gods by so doing, and that death was his punishment. At least it deterred others from following Morcar's example."

"There are many superstitions surrounding the ship, my lord," Wihtlaeg said. "The fishermen say they ofttimes hear voices issuing from the boat-house when there is no one there. The voices, they say, speak in a tongue unknown to them."

"That could well be," Woden said non-committally. "It is good that the fishermen do not understand, and are fearful of approaching the boat-house because they suspect witchcraft. Should they examine the ship, they would not know how to use such knowledge and it could well be a danger to them."

"What knowledge, my lord?"

"The knowledge you will gain when I take you to inspect the ship this evening, my son," Woden said quietly. "You alone shall learn the ship's secrets. The knowledge will give you a wisdom and power denied to lesser mortals, a wisdom and power you will bequeath to your own eldest son."

"I pray I shall be worthy of the confidence you have in me, my lord," Wihtlaeg said earnestly. "Can you tell me of your homeland?"

"It lies many miles from here."

"If only I could visit you there, my lord," Wihtlaeg said wistfully.

Woden smiled. "One day, Wihtlaeg, you shall, I promise you. One day at the ninth hour many years hence when you are old and feel the approach of death, you will find a ship like mine awaiting you on the shore. When that day comes, pass the reins of your chieftainship to your atheling, just as I am doing, have the ship made ready as it will be for my departure, enter the ship with your beloved—if that is as both she and you wish it—and have your people cast you forth into the waters. I shall be waiting for you."

"But what if I am slain in battle, my lord?"

"I shall be waiting for you," repeated Woden insistently.

"But when I am old and nigh unto death, will not you be old also?" asked Wihtlaeg with a puzzled frown.

"The ways of the sky gods are inscrutable, my atheling," Woden said calmly. "I shall be waiting for you."

"What of my brothers and my sister?" Wihtlaeg asked. "When will you tell them of your departure, my lord?"

"I shall not tell them fully, my son," Woden said resolutely. "I shall merely say that their lady mother and I are going on a long visit to my homeland, and that you will be chieftain during my absence. They will naturally assume that we shall return. It is better that they think thus. Only Cerdic and Osbern, my beloved comrades, will share the knowledge with you. I owe them the truth. I know they will serve you as loyally and courageously as they have served me, and their wisdom and experience will be invaluable to you."

"What if my brothers should ask if you will return?"

"They will not ask," Woden said with a smile. "Believe me, they will not ask. Whensoever we say farewell, even to a dying comrade, do we really accept that we shall never see him again? Our reason tells us we shall not, but our heart and our instinct tell us differently. Your brothers will not ask, as you will see, my son."

"My lord, I shall be grief-stricken at your departure, more so than your other children, for I alone shall know the truth," Wihtlaeg said. "But I accept that it is written thus. There is much I do not understand, much that remains hidden from me, but I know that the sky gods will it this way. Is that not so?"

"*Ja*, that is so, my atheling," Woden said gravely. "But the knowledge you will gain when you examine the ship, will increase your understanding and your power."

Woden turned then and going to a great carved chest which stood in the corner of the chamber, he opened it and took out the magnificent sword he had given to Ricole.

"Your lady mother has asked me to give you this," he said, presenting the sword hilt-first to Wihtlaeg. "She could not bring herself to do so."

Wihtlaeg took the sword and examined it closely, fascinated by its exquisite craftsmanship.

" 'Tis fabulously beautiful, my lord," he said wonderingly. "I have never seen its like before."

"It was my *morgengyfu* to your mother and she has held it in trust for you, our first-born," Woden explained. "It is endowed with special attributes. I brought it with me from my homeland. It was the ceremonial sword of my ancestors and has been handed down from father to son for countless generations. It possesses a fatal bite for our enemies and is powerless in their hands, and will now be the defender of you and your line."

"What is the significance of the boar-crested pommel, my lord?" Wihtlaeg asked, curiously.

"The boar crest was wrought to my special requirements

before I left my homeland," Woden answered. "You, my atheling, will be the founder of a new dynasty, and the boar, the Black Boar, will be both your emblem and your protector."

"But surely you are the founder of our line here in Angel, my lord," Wihtlaeg pointed out.

"Nay, my son, I do not belong here," Woden insisted. "You know that. I know that. You will be the first lord of the Black Boar, the first of a long line of chieftains who will rule the Angles with wisdom and justice."

"My lord, you place a great burden of power and responsibility upon me—what if in the years ahead, without you to guide me, my heart fails me?" Wihtlaeg asked, his hero-worship of his father apparent in his boyish gaze. He looked suddenly defenceless as if, after all, his eighteen years lay lightly upon him.

"Always I shall be with you in spirit, my son," Woden said steadily. "When you have need of me, call upon my name. I shall hear you and shall answer the call."

Wihtlaeg's eyes were bright with emotion. "My lord, I swear I shall try to be worthy of you but. . . ." He paused, not trusting himself to speak further.

Woden placed a firm and reassuring hand on one of his son's shoulders.

"In times of personal sorrow and stress, in times of battle when the going is hard, in times when your courage fails and your resolution weakens, call upon the name of Woden," he said with emphasis. "Let that be my last message to my people—the message you, my atheling, shall give them. Let whosoever will, call upon my name and I shall not fail them. As the years pass, the Angles will become a great nation and will people the earth."

"The earth?" asked Wihtlaeg in surprise. "The Angles will one day leave this land of Denmark, my lord?"

Woden's voice was calm and unemotional as he made reply, but his green eyes were those of a visionary.

"Whithersoever my ship doth anchor, shall become their eventual home," he said.

TWENTY-TWO

Most of the inhabitants of Angel were gathering on the shore to watch the departure of their beloved chieftain and his lady. Their lord, who had arrived on the shore in a ship eighteen years earlier, was departing on a visit to his homeland in that very same ship. Loved and respected, he would be sorely missed but his atheling, Wihtlaeg, would take his place as chieftain in his absence. So the Angles told themselves as it approached the ninth hour of the morning and they made their way to the shore.

On the previous evening in the Heorot, Woden and Ricole had held a magnificent banquet for the warriors and their womenfolk. The guests had partaken liberally of steaming dishes of venison, roast pig, roast mutton, and sides of beef, and had drunk copiously of the famed Anglian mead, a spirit fermented from honey and herbs to a recipe of which, it was claimed, only the Angles and the gods knew the secret. The atmosphere in the Heorot had been lively and noisy, the boisterous merriment increasing with every passing hour. But underlying the laughter and merriment, there had been a feeling of sorrow, of *angst*, which no one present, except Wihtlaeg, could properly have explained.

Ever since dawn, under Wihtlaeg's watchful gaze, Woden's other sons, assisted by warriors of the *hearth-horde*, had been loading articles—the departing couple's personal possessions and the many beautiful leaving-presents which had been given to them during the feast—on to the ship. Amongst these articles, was a gold-mounted shield presented to Woden by Cerdic in symbol of his office as leader of the *hearth-horde*; a sword with a gold and garnet pommel presented by Osbern as a symbol of his office as deputy leader of the *hearth-horde*; four spears and three javelins each presented by a member of the *hearth-horde*; an iron-handled axe from Ceolburh and her Olaf; a pair of hinged and curved epaulets from the twins Baeldaeg and Waegdaeg; a gold buckle weighing fifteen ounces from Wyrt; a great whetstone, two feet long and carved with bearded faces presented by the carpenters of Angel; and a wrought iron standard, surmounted by Seaxwulf's emblem, a stag, sent to Woden as a goodwill gesture by the Saxon chieftain. These, and many other treasures including Woden's regalia, were cached amidships.

At last, as it neared the ninth hour, all was ready for departure.

Woden and Ricole took their leave of their children in the privacy of their dwelling. Woden was dressed as a warrior, in a coat of mail covered by a long circular cloak. He wore gold bracelets and rings and carried his gold helmet. Ricole was wearing a red woollen gown fastened at the bodice with three jewelled brooches, which were looped together with festoons of glass and amber beads. T-shaped trinkets and small ivory rings hung from her girdle, as well as her small knife. She wore a long cloak and head-rail and carried a purse, its top exquisitely decorated with seven ornamental plaques, which was Wihtlaeg's parting gift to her.

Ricole made a valiant effort to hold back her tears as she bade her children farewell. Her heart ached as she hugged her small daughter for the last time but Nigon, holding Ceolburh's hand and unaware of the poignancy of the moment, turned away to stare in wide-eyed fascination at Ceolburh who had suddenly burst into tears.

Woden and Ricole embraced their sons in farewell and, strangely, it was only Wihtlaeg who showed emotion—briefly, as he spoke to his father.

"Farewell, my lord," he said with a catch in his voice. "Be assured I shall not fail you. May the gods who have called you bid you welcome."

Her own eyes brimming with tears, Ricole registered the fact that Woden made no reply. He clasped Wihtlaeg's shoulder firmly and affectionately. His features were as controlled as ever but it was apparent that he did not trust himself to speak.

Woden turned then and taking Ricole's hand, led her from the dwelling. Accompanied by their children, they made their way to the shore along a route lined with people. To the accompaniment of cheers of encouragement, of shouts such as: "Safe journey, my lord!" "Freya protect you, my lady!" and "May the gods bring you safely back to us, my lord, my lady!", they crossed the shore to the water's edge.

The spacious ship with its curved prow stood ready on the shore; laden with treasure, it rode at anchor, awaiting their arrival. Was ever a ship equipped more handsomely with weapons and war-gear, swords and corslets? Already Huginn, the raven, was in his place, perched on the ship's prow.

Woden helped Ricole into the ship, where she seated herself opposite him, facing the shore, that she might look upon the faces of her loved ones until they receded from view.

At Woden's signal, men waded into the water, released the mooring ropes and cast the ship off into the waters of the estuary. It drew away from the shore slowly at first and the watching Angles fell silent, watching intently. But then, unaided by sail or oars, it surged suddenly forward, sweeping over the waves and foaming at the bows. At this point, a great cheer went up from the shore.

"Look, my lord!" Ricole said suddenly. "A bird, a raven, has just left the shore and is flying towards us."

Woden smiled but did not look round.

"So Muninn, too, has made her decision," he said.

"Muninn? What do you mean, my lord?"

"See, little one, she has caught up with us now and has perched herself on the prow beside Huginn."

"Huginn is rumpling her feathers with his beak, as if to say 'Welcome aboard!'" Ricole said, with a catch in her voice. "I see what you mean, my lord—Muninn, too, has left her children."

The ship was moving faster now, heading towards the mouth of the estuary and the open sea, butting the waves as it entered deeper waters. The faces of the people on the shore would soon be indistinguishable.

Two cries from the shore rent the air then, coming plainly across the sparkling waters. Cries of affection and of lamentation, they were the cries of a people whose hearts were grieving, whose minds were mourning.

"Wo...o...o...den! Wo...o...o...den!"

Woden did not look back. He gazed straight ahead as if he were concentrating his mind and energies on the journey ahead, as if Angel were the past and he were looking to the future.

Ricole, her gaze never leaving the shore, saw Wihtlaeg bend down and lift little Nigon in his arms. The child buried her face against his shoulder as if she were weeping. Ricole's own eyes filled with tears and she looked agonisedly at Woden.

She looked at Woden and her gaze was held by what she saw. Woden was facing the morning sun and seemed to be illuminated by its golden rays. His face was shining with beauty and with love. At once Ricole's sorrow dissolved into nothingness, to be replaced by joy and contentment. She continued to gaze at Woden, as though already she had forgotten the figures on the shore, until the ship reached the open sea and the figures had disappeared over the horizon.

Woden leaned forward and pressed one of the knobs on the panel below the rowlocks. . . .

*   *   *

The Angles on the shore strained their eyes to catch a last glimpse of the ship as it reached the mouth of the estuary and approached the open sea. They watched intently, shielding their eyes against the sunlight, until the ship neared the horizon.

But then they could see no more. Uneasy and apprehensive, the chattering throng fell silent, for darkness was descending on Angel—just as it had done at the time of Woden's arrival. In a few moments utter darkness had again covered the earth.

"Holy goddess! Is it possible, Baeldaeg?" Waegdaeg called to his twin from the blackness. "In a few seconds it has changed from daylight to nightfall."

"Look there, brother!" Baeldaeg exclaimed, clutching Waegdaeg's shoulder excitedly. "Is not that the star comet of which the priests and wisemen speak?"

"The star comet?" Waegdaeg answered. "It looks more like a ball of fire to me."

"People mention a ball of fire, brother, when they speak of our lord father's arrival here."

All gazed at the curious phenomenon, the disc-like object which looked in its dazzling brilliance like a fast-moving sun in a starlit sky. But there was no sun. There were no stars. There was no light. There was only a ball of fire and total darkness.

"By Frigg!" exclaimed Waegdaeg in surprise. "The comet, if it is a comet, is whirling towards the earth at a terrific speed."

"Towards the earth you say?" asked Baeldaeg doubtfully. " 'Tis difficult to be certain in the darkness but it looks to me to be coming down over the sea."

"Look, brother! Loki's bones, did you mark that?" asked Waegdaeg in wonderment.

"*Ja*, the comet dropped right down to the earth, remained stationary for a few seconds, and now it is rising up into the sky. . . ."

"And now it has disappeared!" complained Waegdaeg. "There is no sign of it anywhere."

"You need not sound so disappointed," chuckled Baeldaeg. "See, brother, 'tis getting light again! Blood of the gods! In just a few seconds, daylight has returned and there's bright sunshine all around us!"

Craning their necks and narrowing their eyes against the sudden brilliance, the people on the shore gazed once more into the distance. This time the horizon was empty.

Bewildered and sorrowful that the eclipse had robbed them of a last sight of their departing lord and his lady, all turned to Wihtlaeg for consolation and guidance.

But Wihtlaeg, holding little Nigon against his shoulder, looked confident and relaxed.

"The sea is empty," Baeldaeg said to him, with a catch in his voice. "They have gone."

Wihtlaeg shook his head. "Nay, my brother, they are still there," he said firmly.

"Then you must have been blessed with longer sight than us, my lord Wihtlaeg," Waegdaeg said, agreeing as always with his twin. "Baeldaeg and I cannot see them."

"Will our lord father ever return?" asked Wyrt gloomily, his poetic soul stricken with grief. "I wanted to ask him that question but I could not bring myself to do so. My mind tells me this is a final farewell, but my heart and my instinct tell me differently."

Wihtlaeg turned to his brothers. He spoke in a voice that could be heard by all those who were crowding round him on the shore. His voice was calm and reassuring.

"Our lord, the mighty Woden, is still there," he said. "He has but crossed the horizon, the limit of our sight."

ENVOI

In A.D. 1939, excavations at Sutton Hoo, an estate in East Anglia, brought to light an Anglo-Saxon ship buried in the sand. The ship's timbers had rotted away, but their impression in the sand and the iron rivets that remained showed it to be an eighty foot long, mastless, clinker-built rowboat.

Richly ornamented grave goods were cached amidships, and included a gold-mounted shield, a sword with a gold and garnet pommel, a coat of mail, a visored helmet enriched with gold inlay, an iron-handled axe, four spears, three javelins, and a small knife. There were forty-one items of solid gold, all richly decorated with garnets, including a magnificent purse top decorated with seven ornamental plaques, buckles and strap mounts, a pair of hinged and curved epaulets, pyramid studs for the sword knot, buttons, and a gold buckle weighing fifteen ounces.

A great whetstone, two feet long and carved with bearded faces, and a wrought iron standard surmounted with a stag, were both ceremonial objects and indicated that the deceased had been a prince.

Thought to be a royal burial ship, there was no sign of a body or cremated remains; and nothing to indicate—if it were a monument erected to one buried elsewhere—whose cenotaph it was.

It was a burial ship without a corpse; a ship either ritually buried in the sand, or washed up, many centuries before, on the east coast of Britain. The richest Teutonic find in Europe since the seventeenth century, the Sutton Hoo ship, despite its priceless treasure, baffled the archaeologists. Its mystery remains, and will always remain, unsolved.

To whom did the uninhabited ship belong? Did it once contain a body—or bodies? If so, what became of them? Whence came the ship? Did it lie in its last resting-place by accident or design? Why were such fabulous grave goods buried in an otherwise deserted ship? Could it have been a memorial to one of the Anglian kings of East Anglia? Was it a memorial to King Aethelhere who died fighting for Penda, the pagan King of Mercia? Aethelhere's body, drowned in the River Winwaed, was not recovered from the battle. Or was it a memorial to King Anna, a notable Christian, who was buried at Blythburgh in Suffolk? Was the burial ship intended to placate his heathen followers?

Many are the questions. Many are the theories. As always, there is only one answer.

What was that you said, my friend? You believe you know the answer? In Woden's name, you could well be right!